SPACE ODDITIES

Short Stories of Time, Space and Possibility

Gareth Davies

Spiralix Publishing

SPIRALIX
PUBLISHING

ISBN: 979-8-26-710052-6

Space is big. Really big. You just won't believe how vastly, hugely, mind-bogglingly big it is. I mean, you may think it's a long way down the road to the chemist's, but that's just peanuts to space

DOUGLAS ADAMS, THE HITCHHIKER'S GUIDE TO THE GALAXY

CONTENTS

INTRODUCTION

At the Edges of Reality

T he universe is far bigger than we can imagine. Not just in distance, not just in scale, but in concept. When we lift our eyes to the stars, we sense something vast, but our instincts are poor guides. What seems like an endless sky is only the faintest hint of what stretches beyond. Galaxies lie like grains of sand scattered across a dark beach, and beyond them more galaxies, and still more beyond that, into distances where numbers strain and meaning frays.

Yet size is not the strangest thing about the cosmos. Its true peculiarity lies in its rules. Space and time do not stand apart, but intertwine into a single, pliable fabric: spacetime. Mass bends it, gravity flows through it, and light itself curves to its shape. We are taught to think of time as a river, but relativity insists it is more like a landscape. Travel fast enough or near enough to something massive, and the flow of seconds twists into something alien, where one person's minute is another's year.

On the smallest scales, the world grows stranger still. Quantum physics tells us that particles do not behave like marbles or billiard balls. They spread into probabilities, they interfere with themselves, they vanish and reappear. An electron does not travel from point A to point B along a line, it explores every possible path and only when we look does it seem to have chosen one. This is not a trick of language or metaphor. The mathematics that describes this behaviour is exact and predictive and yet it describes a world utterly unlike our common sense.

We therefore find ourselves in a curious position. We live in a universe where the foundations of reality resist simple understanding. Our experiments confirm what our minds resist. Particles are in many places at once until observed. Empty space teems with energy. Time itself is elastic. The rules of existence are written in paradox, and yet they hold the stars in place and power the electronics in our pockets.

The stories in Spacetime Oddities grow out of this tension, the gap between what science has shown and what our imaginations can contain. They worry at the edges of knowledge, prising apart the seams of physics to ask, "What if?" What if the quirks of quantum mechanics scaled up into the macroscopic world? What if the curvature of spacetime was not a distant abstraction but a lived reality? What if the limits we treat as fixed, past and future, here and there, matter and energy, were not limits at all, but boundaries we might cross with a thought, a machine, or a mistake?

These are not tales of faster-than-light starships or alien empires. They are thought experiments, built into stories.

Each one takes a scientific oddity, something our best theories already whisper to us is true, and turns it sideways. They are explorations, not of distant galaxies, but of the uncanny possibilities hidden in the rules of the universe we already inhabit.

In these pages, space and time are shuffled like cards. Quantum particles bloom into everyday objects. Energy is harvested from the fabric of reality itself. An alien artefact bends the meaning of "up" and "tomorrow." Scientists prod at primordial black holes, only to discover that what seems tiny may control vast forces. These are stories of people, curious, reckless, brilliant and flawed, set against the backdrop of a cosmos stranger than fiction, where each discovery leads to another, and certainty is never guaranteed.

Because here is the deepest oddity of all. The universe is not obliged to make sense to us. It is not built for our comfort or designed to fit our expectations. It is immense, alien, beautiful and terrifying. Yet, by asking questions, by peering into the cracks, by following our curiosity wherever it leads, we can glimpse its workings. Stories like these are one way of doing that. Stories of testing in imagination, what it might be like to live with truths so strange they defy belief.

Step across the threshold and set aside the everyday certainties of cause and effect, of up and down, of before and after. Enter a space where reality is provisional, where observation shapes existence, where the possible is wider than we dare to admit. These are the Spacetime Oddities.

Never forget that sometimes, the strangest discoveries are not out there among the stars, but right here, hidden in the rules we thought we already understood.

1. THE WORLD WE SEE

Human perception is limited: our eyes capture only a sliver of the spectrum, our ears register a narrow band of vibrations, our minds construct a world from fragments. Science has long revealed how much lies beyond us such as invisible wavelengths, microscopic life and distant galaxies. Yet all these things exist whether we notice them or not. Or do they?

.~.

T aren was not a farmer, though he tilled his allotted strip of land. He was not a craftsman, though his hands could mend a tool or carve a beam. He was, by necessity, part of the village but his heart was always elsewhere.

Where others saw chores, Taren saw horizons. He would finish his work as quickly as possible and slip away, climbing the low rise beyond the fields, straying into meadows or thickets, following the winding course of the river. His neighbours muttered about his restlessness. Some called him lazy, others distracted. A few shook their heads in pity. But Taren felt only that something in the world was unfinished. It was like a story missing its middle chapters, or a painting whose corners still waited for colour.

One morning when the air was cool and the ground damp with dew, Taren climbed the rise again. The earth there had always been a patchwork of soil and stone, bare save for grass and thorn. Yet as the light grew, he noticed shapes he had never seen before. He stopped, heart quickening.

Thin, delicate flares tipped with colour startled the eye, rising from the green stalks as if to greet him. He stared, bewildered. They had not been there yesterday. He was certain of it. He knew every stone of this slope, had crossed it dozens of times. Now it was adorned with softness and colour, as if a painter had worked overnight.

As he looked, a word arrived in his mind: *flower*.

It landed with such force that he almost spoke it aloud. He had never heard it before, yet now it seemed inevitable, the only word that could possibly name what stood before him. Along with it came others: *petal, stem, leaf.* They felt as natural as breath.

Taren knelt and touched one of the blossoms. It was fragile, cool and impossibly real. A tremor ran through him. It was not simply that the plant had appeared overnight. It was that the idea and the name had arrived with it. Yesterday, he would not even have known what to call it. He walked back to the village dazed, clutching a single bloom. He told no one. The thought of explaining that both thing and thought had appeared together seemed absurd. Who would believe him?

.~.

The next day, he returned. More blossoms appeared, spreading across the rise. Some were yellow, others purple, others white. They stood in clusters, bending in the wind. Each time he fixed his gaze on a new detail, a word sprang to mind: *root, pollen, fragrance.* His mind was being furnished at the same time as the land was being adorned.

He tried to ignore it, to work his fields and carry his water like everyone else. But the knowledge that the world was incomplete without him gnawed at him. He could not keep it inside forever.

At last, he told Mira.

She was at the well, her sleeves rolled to her elbows, her jug brimming. Mira was steady and calm where Taren was restless, thoughtful where he was impulsive. She listened to people, even when they rambled, and her gaze often wandered beyond the rooftops as though horizons spoke to her too.

"I want to show you something," Taren said, his voice low. He unwrapped the bloom he had pressed between two pieces of cloth.

Mira tilted her head. "What's it called?"

Taren hesitated, then said, "Flower."

Mira repeated it softly. Her eyes widened as if she had never heard the sound before and yet, as she spoke it, the word became solid and natural. She blinked and looked up at him. "Did you know that yesterday?"

"No. The word came when I saw it. As though it was given with the thing itself."

Mira studied the bloom again. For a long time she was silent. Then she nodded. "Show me."

That evening, they climbed the rise together. The blossoms stirred in the breeze, nodding their heads. Mira knelt, her eyes widening as she looked closely. "Petal," she murmured. "Stem. Leaf." She touched one gently, as if afraid it might vanish. "They weren't here before."

"No," Taren said. "The world waits until we notice."

.~.

From that day, they explored side by side. Taren and Mira wandered along the riverbank, their feet brushing damp grass and scattered stones. Each day revealed something new, though yesterday's world had seemed so complete. Now, every glance brought small wonders to light: clusters of moss that shimmered faintly in the morning dew, tiny insects glinting with iridescence, and mushrooms curling in shapes neither had seen before.

Taren paused to watch a droplet sliding along a blade of grass. Its path carved a tiny rivulet in the soil, curling softly around a pebble and, as he followed it with his eyes, he felt a word coalesce in his mind: *trace.* Mira knelt beside him, touching the soil gently. "Trace," she whispered. "The movement. it leaves a mark."

Further along, petals and stems appeared along the river's edge. Their colours startled Taren's eye. Deep crimson, violet, yellow and white. As he gazed, the words arrived again: *petal, stem, leaf.* Each word felt like a natural extension of the shapes themselves. Mira traced a finger along a curled petal, noting the way it twisted softly toward the sun. Another word blossomed in her mind: *curl.*

Even the river seemed to respond to their attention. Gentle ripples formed arcs and eddies, some reflecting sunlight, others casting subtle shadows on the riverbed. Tiny fish appeared, darting in and out of sight, leaving behind patterns of movement that had no name until, as Taren studied them closely, the words came: *dart, shimmer, glide.*

At one spot, a fallen leaf spun slowly on the surface, tracing a miniature spiral. Taren watched, fascinated, as the curve repeated itself in smaller eddies, a pattern almost too small to see. Mira's gaze followed, and she whispered: "It's like it wants to grow, to twist further than we can yet notice." Even the smallest details seemed to echo larger forms, hinting at patterns beyond their comprehension.

.~.

As evening fell, they reached a bend in the river Taren had always crossed without thought. The water here was still, yet as the last light lingered, a movement caught his eye. A swirl of floating petals traced a delicate curve, drifting slowly with the current. He crouched closer.

At first, it seemed a simple spiral, elegant but unremarkable. Then he noticed smaller spirals forming within it: leaves curling, tiny eddies spinning, and water patterns mirroring the motion in miniature. Each sub-spiral echoed the larger one, repeating infinitely, fractal in its complexity.

Mira gasped. "It's alive," she whispered. "Not just the flowers, not just the water. The spiral itself grows as we watch."

The sky above shifted with similar subtlety. Stars appeared as faint pinpricks, then constellations traced themselves into patterns they could suddenly recognise: *arc, cluster, horizon.* Each time they named a detail, the world around them deepened in richness. It was as if seeing was itself a form of creation, and even the tiniest curl, the softest twist, carried the promise of something greater yet unseen. The curl, the spiral, was a living pattern, infinitely replicating, a microcosm of the world itself.

They lingered, mesmerised, letting the river and its fractal pattern wash over them. Neither spoke; words felt too crude for what they were witnessing. At last, Taren reached for Mira's hand, and together they stepped back, carrying the memory of the spiral with them.

Taren's heart quickened. Every detail, every petal, fish and star, seemed to respond to their attention, revealing layers of hidden structure.

Every glance afterward felt charged with potential. The world, they realised, was a tapestry still being woven, each observation adding a new thread. They returned to the village quietly, hearts and thoughts expanded, knowing that what they had seen at the river bend was only the beginning That the universe itself was waiting to reveal its wonders to those willing to notice.

.~.

At first, they kept this secret between them. But whispers spread. A child saw the pressed flower in Mira's hand and gasped. Others followed them up the rise, curious. Some scoffed. "A weed's a weed, no matter what fancy word you give it." Others grew uneasy. "It's dangerous to meddle with what's already made."

Yet more were curious. And when they looked for themselves, they could not deny what they saw.

One night, Taren and Mira gathered a small group to watch the stars. They pointed out a cluster that had not been visible before. As they named it, more stars seemed to ignite in the gaps. The group murmured in awe. One youth cried out suddenly, pointing to a hazy glow on the horizon. "Galaxy!" The word arrived in all their minds at once, and they knew it as surely as their own names.

From then, exploration became a village obsession. Children brought home new kinds of leaves and pebbles, each with names that seemed to spring into their thoughts as they examined them. Elders began to keep records, drawing careful sketches and labelling them.

The village library, once a bare hall with only a handful of scrolls, began to change. Where shelves had been empty, books now stood. No one had written them, yet when opened, they contained diagrams, charts, and descriptions that matched the newest discoveries.

"It's as though the books write themselves," Mira whispered to Taren one evening.

"Or as though they were always waiting," he replied.

Craftsmen built instruments to aid the explorations. Polished glass discs brought the distant stars closer. Water clocks measured the passage of time with new precision. Tall wooden towers were raised to peer beyond the village boundary and with each tool, more detail emerged.

Boats were built to follow the widening river downstream. When they sailed, new landscapes unfolded. Forests of towering trees, shores alive with creatures never seen before. Every arrival was accompanied by knowledge. The word *harbour* as they pulled into a cove, *compass* as they noticed the pull of lodestones, *tide* as the waters rose and fell.

The villagers began to speak differently. Their conversations filled with new words, new ideas. Where once they had spoken only of crops and seasons, now they debated *orbit, distance, angle.* They no longer saw themselves as a small cluster of people in a fixed valley, but as explorers in an unfolding universe.

Not everyone welcomed it. Some muttered that too much curiosity would summon trouble. One elder stood in the square and declared, "If the world has no end, then leave it alone! What if we find something that should not be?"

But most were captivated. The more they looked, the richer the world became.

.~.

As years passed, the village became a centre of wonder and inquiry. Observation was no longer a pastime, it had become a philosophy. Scholars debated what it meant to exist. Were objects dependent on sight, or did observation merely reveal them? Some argued that the universe was fragile, waiting for attention to stabilise its forms. Others believed it was a companion, inviting discovery with trust and patience. A few suggested that even people themselves were unfinished until observed by others.

The younger generation, raised in this world of emergent detail, explored eagerly. They measured clouds and wind, sketched river patterns, recorded the shimmer of insects and the subtle music of blossoms. Instruments became more sophisticated: telescopes revealed distant galaxies, water clocks marked seconds with precise mechanisms, and polished lenses magnified the veins of leaves or the spiral of shells.

The arts flourished. Painters learned to capture ephemeral patterns: the quiver of a petal, the glint of a pebble, the shimmer of morning dew. Musicians translated wind and birdcall into melodies. Storytellers described events that had never been seen until someone looked closely enough to witness them, and the words themselves carried the shapes and textures they named.

10

Knowledge grew organically, yet remained entwined with perception. Observation shaped reality, and reality inspired new observation. The village, once small and inward-looking, expanded in thought and imagination.

Taren and Mira guided this growth gently, encouraging exploration without dominating it. Villagers built boats to follow the river, mapping previously blank lands. Forests revealed towering trees, rivers teemed with fish, hidden coves became harbours, all stabilised by careful observation.

Libraries filled with self-writing books: diagrams of leaves, river eddies, stars, animal movements, and architectural designs. Instruments brought the invisible into focus: microscopes revealed tiny patterns in soil and water, telescopes exposed distant planets, polished lenses magnified snowflakes, veins of leaves, and the shimmer of insects.

The village became a hub of collective discovery. Elders taught attentive observation. Children recorded new forms, sounds, and patterns. Artisans built tools to magnify, measure, and replicate details. Words proliferated alongside phenomena: *prism, reflection, eddy, ripple, spiral, thread.* Every named observation anchored reality.

Even social life evolved. Conversations once dominated by crops and seasons now included debate about the emerging world about them. Communities measured time in hours, minutes, and seconds; mapped the river's course; observed celestial motions. Observation had become the foundation of culture, connecting people to each other and to the universe in an active, creative dialogue.

Generations passed. Wooden towers became stone observatories. The village grew into a town, then a city. Streets were lined with instruments, libraries, and workshops. Ships explored oceans once blank on maps. New continents appeared, waiting for explorers to witness and name them. Science, art, philosophy and exploration were inseparable, each feeding the other.

.~.

Taren and Mira, by now elders, walked together once more to the rise where it had begun. Their hair was silver, hands lined with decades of labour and curiosity. The slope had transformed into a vast tapestry of life: flowers of hundreds of varieties, mosses that shimmered like gemstones, small mammals and birds that emerged only when attention lingered, rivers twisting in elaborate spirals. Above, the night sky stretched endlessly. Galaxies and nebulae forming a living tapestry of light.

Mira leaned on her staff, eyes reflecting the stars. "Do you think it will ever end?" she asked softly.

Taren smiled faintly, eyes bright with wonder. "Only if we choose to stop. The universe is endless so long as we keep asking."

They paused, letting the wind carry the hum of insects, the rustle of leaves, the faint music of distant waterfalls. Even shadows, moving slowly across the ground, could be divided into hours, minutes, and seconds when they chose to observe. Everything was alive with detail, layered and expanding, awaiting attention to become fully realised.

"Even thought changes when we dare to look," Taren murmured.

Mira nodded, tracing a dew-laden leaf. "Even we are unfinished until seen by each other," she added.

Hand in hand, they gazed across the meadow. Every blossom, pebble, star, and ripple was testimony to generations of attention, curiosity, and wonder. The universe had become a shared creation, evolving with each observer, growing richer with every named detail.

They stood quietly as the stars blazed above. The rise, once bare, was now a microcosm of the cosmos. A living record of discovery, perception, and care. The world we see is the gift still unfolding page by page, word by word, as long as eyes dare to look.

2. TURN LEFT
TO YESTERDAY

Physics treats space and time as part of the same fabric, called 'spacetime'. A four-dimensional grid where the three familiar directions combine with the one we call "past to future". In principle those axes can be described mathematically like any others. They can bend and stretch. Even rotate.

What if one of those rotations were not just theory but reality? What if the left-right of our everyday movements were swapped with the flow of time itself so that turning a corner might not take you down another street but send you a step into yesterday or tomorrow?

.~.

D r Elias Roe stood in the middle of his lab, chalk dust on his cuffs and a smudge of graphite across his cheek. The device on the bench hummed faintly, its coils bright with charge. He checked the dials again. His lips moving as he repeated the numbers under his breath.

Miriam Khouri leaned against the doorway with arms folded. "You've been at it since dawn. What are you expecting this time?"

"Confirmation," Roe said. "A rotation of the grid. If time and space are axes, why shouldn't they turn?"

"You've tried bending them before. What's different now?"

He tapped the glass tube at the centre of the frame. "Precision. If I shift left and right onto earlier and later, the effect will show here first. It only needs the smallest nudge."

Miriam frowned. "You want to trade direction for time?"

"Yes. For centuries we've assumed time is one way only but the equations never insist on that. They allow for change. Even reversal."

She glanced at the blackboard behind him with lines of symbols crowding the surface. "Equations are safe. The city outside isn't."

Roe didn't answer. He gripped the main switch and pulled it down. The coils lit and hummed louder. A tremor passed through the floor. Chalk rolled across the bench.

At first there was nothing. Roe's shoulders sagged. Then he noticed his coffee mug sliding toward the left edge. He reached to stop it but his hand closed on air. The mug sat in front of him again already drained. A moment earlier it had been full.

Miriam straightened. "What did you just do?"

He stared at the mug. "I mapped left onto earlier. Moving in that direction now displaces you in time."

"You're saying the mug went into the past?"

"Yes. Only seconds but it proves the principle." His eyes were bright with excitement. "We're no longer bound by the separation of directions. Left is yesterday. Right could be tomorrow."

Miriam shook her head. "That isn't just theory anymore. If this spreads people will feel it."

Roe was already writing in his notebook and recording the displacement. The lines of chalk dust still trembled on the bench as if the air itself had been unsettled.

Miriam stepped closer. "Elias, do you realise what you've

done? If the grid has shifted, every turn anyone makes could throw them out of sync."

He didn't look up. "That's what I need to measure. If the axis holds then we can predict the effect. Perhaps even control it."

Her voice sharpened. "Control? You've just sent a coffee mug into yesterday."

Roe snapped the notebook shut. "Yes. Which means it worked."

The machine's hum softened leaving the room strangely still. Outside, through the tall windows, the street seemed ordinary. Pedestrians walked and traffic rolled past. But Roe felt it already. A tilt, subtle and invisible, stretching beneath everything familiar.

Miriam followed his gaze. "Do you think they'll notice?"

"They will," he said. "Soon."

.~.

The machine had gone silent but Roe and Miriam knew the effect was not contained. By late morning they were out on the street watching for signs. At first everything looked normal with shopfronts open, buses grinding along their routes and schoolchildren walking in pairs. Yet the details soon betrayed themselves.

At the corner café, a waiter carried a tray of cups. He stepped left to avoid a chair and the tray vanished from his hands. A moment later it stood on the counter already empty. The waiter blinked and glanced at his palms in confusion.

Miriam touched Roe's sleeve. "Did you see that? He moved sideways and jumped into yesterday."

Roe's jaw tightened. "Not jumped. Slipped. Left is no longer space. It's earlier."

They walked on, their pace cautious. At a bookshop, a girl picked up a book with her left hand but as she went to open it, the book was suddenly back on the shelf exactly where it had been before. She turned away, unsettled.

15

"This isn't just objects," Miriam whispered. "It's people too. Every turn they take risks pulling them out of order."

Across the street, a bus swung left into an avenue. Its rear wheels lagged, then the whole vehicle flickered out and reappeared halfway down the road with the passengers rattled but intact. The driver pulled over and shook his head.

Roe scribbled notes as fast as he could. "Consistent pattern. Each leftward motion equals a displacement into the past. Seconds only but enough to be seen."

Miriam caught his wrist. "Elias, stop writing. Look at them. Nobody knows what's happening. They think they're losing their minds."

He glanced up. A woman on the pavement clutched her handbag, staring at her watch as the second hand slipped back before resuming. A cyclist swerved left around a lamppost and reappeared behind the same lamppost, tyres squealing.

A boy ran from the bakery with a paper bag. He turned left and vanished, bag and all. His mother cried out. Then he was back at the bakery door holding the bag but looking shaken as though he had relived the last seconds in reverse.

Miriam's face hardened. "This isn't theory anymore. It's chaos."

Nancy Holt's taxi screeched to a halt beside them and her horn blared. She leaned out of the window, her tone sharp. "Doc, what's going on? I take a left turn and I'm dropping passengers off before they've even paid. Straight roads are fine but corners are a nightmare. Fix it!"

Roe closed his notebook slowly. "The machine rotated the axes. The grid's tilted. Left and right aren't directions anymore. They're times."

Nancy glared. "Then put them back." She slammed the gearstick into drive and pulled away.

Miriam turned to Roe. "She's right. You can't leave it like this. Shops can't function. Schools can't function. The whole city will unravel."

Roe stood still for a moment, the noise of traffic and voices folding around him. Every action carried an echo now. Left meant a stumble into yesterday. Right, he suspected, would soon reach forward. His test had been too effective.

Miriam's voice cut in again, quieter now. "You said you wanted confirmation. Well, here it is. You've proved the idea. But proof is not worth this."

He looked at her, then down at his notes. The neat columns of times and displacements had become something heavier. Evidence of disruption, not discovery.

"You're right," he said at last. "It has to be undone."

They stood together at the corner, watching the street stutter and sway as if time itself were poorly laid cobblestones. For the first time, Roe felt not the pride of an experiment but the weight of responsibility.

.~.

By midday the city was unsettled. Traffic lights flicked in order but cars did not obey them. A bus would half-turn then vanish then reappear further back on the road. Pedestrians walked with caution, afraid to step left at all. The air itself felt strained as though every movement carried a hidden cost.

Roe and Miriam reached the park. Children were playing football on the grass with their shouts loud in the uneasy stillness. A boy kicked the ball left. It blinked out then reappeared seconds earlier at his feet. His boot swung through empty air. The boy froze.

"They've started noticing," Miriam said.

Another child tried a shot. The ball leapt forward then landed ahead of time, bouncing before his leg had even finished the kick. The children chased after it, confused, laughing but also afraid. Parents called them back unsure of what they were seeing.

Roe's eyes followed every motion. "This confirms it. Left is always earlier, right always later. The displacement is consistent. Seconds at most but unmistakable."

Miriam shook her head. "You make it sound like data. They're children, Elias. They don't understand why their game doesn't work."

A cyclist veered to avoid the group and swerved left. He vanished behind a tree and reappeared before he had reached it. His front wheel buckled sending him crashing to the path. People rushed to help him, bewildered.

Roe scribbled in his notebook marking down times and positions. His expression was intent almost feverish.

"Elias, stop," Miriam said sharply. "It's not an experiment anymore. People are frightened. Look around you."

Across the park, a woman stepped sideways with a pram. For an instant she was back where she had started and her face was pale with shock. A dog chasing a stick disappeared mid-leap then landed before its owner had thrown.

Nancy's taxi pulled up at the kerb with a squeal of brakes. She leaned out, eyes blazing. "It's worse every block. I turned left by the station and ended up outside the school five minutes earlier. Passengers are yelling at me. I can't drive like this."

Roe glanced up from his notes. "The effect has spread further than I thought. It's not local anymore."

"No kidding," Nancy snapped. "You did this so undo it!" She pulled away in a screech of tyres.

Miriam stepped in front of Roe, blocking his view of the football match. "Listen to her. You wanted to see if it could be done. You've seen it. Now you have to stop it."

He hesitated with his notebook still open. The figures stared back at him neat and clear but the park was full of disordered movement. Children shouting in confusion, parents calling them away, cyclists on the ground, drivers abandoning cars. The evidence was no longer academic.

"I didn't expect it to spread this fast," he said at last. His voice was low and almost swallowed by the noise of the park. "The whole grid has tilted. The change is everywhere."

Miriam's tone softened. "Then you know what has to happen. You can't leave the city like this."

Roe closed the notebook. The sound of it shutting felt final like the end of a chapter. For the first time he allowed himself to admit what Miriam had been saying all along.

"I'll take responsibility," he said. "I'll put it back."

.~.

The laboratory was filled with the steady thrum of the machine. Glass tubes glowed faintly, throwing shadows across chalkboards crowded with equations. Roe stood over the console, pencil in hand, while Miriam lingered near the door.

"You've seen enough," she said. "The city is tearing itself apart. You need to put it back. Now!"

"I can't just switch it off," Roe replied. "If I do, the misalignment will stay frozen in place. We need to map the distortions first."

Miriam crossed the room. "Mapping won't help the people outside. They're afraid. Shops can't run, buses can't turn. Even walking feels dangerous."

He gestured to the graphs spread across the bench. "Every displacement follows the same grid. If left leads into the past and right into the future then each action leaves a trace. Once we know the pattern, we can rotate the axes back into alignment."

On the screen above the machine, lines traced across a map of the city. Small loops marked the places where children's footballs had flickered. Larger displacements lit up intersections where buses had jumped through time. All of them fed into a central zone of distortion.

"That's the source," Roe said, pointing. "The axis is rotated around this point. If I reverse it there then the rest will naturally follow."

Miriam studied the map unsettled by the constant flickering. "And if you misjudge?"

"Then time remains broken," Roe said flatly. "But we have no choice."

He entered the measurements from his notebook. The machine responded with a rising hum. On the screen, the loops tightened slightly. In the park, a football rolled a fraction more smoothly before shuddering back into confusion.

Miriam leaned close. "You're testing it already?"

"A small correction. I had to see if the system responds." He tapped the glass. "It does."

She exhaled. "So you really can undo it."

"Yes. But it must be exact. A miscalibration could make it worse."

Miriam placed a hand on his arm. "Then be sure. Because this isn't just physics anymore. It's people's lives."

Roe nodded once. He turned back to the bench, set his notes in order then marked the core adjustment. His pencil hovered for a moment before he pressed it to the page. "We'll begin at the centre then move outward. Step by step until left and right are space again."

The machine's hum deepened as he recalibrated the first settings. Lights flickered across the display and for a moment the map of the city seemed to settle. Cars traced smoother paths, pedestrians walked with fewer jolts. Then the image shook, waiting for the final command.

Miriam studied Roe's face. "You wanted proof and you have it. Now you have to accept what that proof cost. Now, fix it."

Roe closed the notebook. "Yes. It's mine to fix."

.~.

He turned to the console. His hands moved with care, adjusting dials and checking calibrations. The machine's hum deepened as he prepared the sequence.

Miriam watched in silence. "You'll need the same precision that started this. No mistakes."

"There won't be." Roe paused with his hand over the main lever. "The misalignment followed the rules of the grid. That means it can be reversed the same way. Straightened. Restored."

Miriam touched his arm. "Don't forget what drove you to this in the first place. It wasn't about breaking the world. It was about understanding it."

"I remember," he said. "Now I understand more than I wanted."

The machine glowed brighter, waiting for his command. Roe looked down once at the notebook and then at the console.

"Step by step," he said. "That's how we bring it back."

.~.

The lab shook with the low hum of the machine. Coils glowed with a steady light, arcs sparking inside the glass cylinders. Roe stood over the console with notebook open and Miriam at his side.

"This is where it ends," he said. "We map the rotation back into a straight line. Left becomes space again. Time resumes its flow."

Miriam nodded, though her hands were tight on the edge of the bench. "Then do it. But be sure."

Roe set the coordinates, guided by the measurements he had gathered since morning. Each number marked a point where the grid had slipped. Each adjustment aimed at drawing it back into place. He pulled the lever. The hum deepened and pressed against their chests.

On the screen above, the flickering map of the city began to shift. Disruptions contracted as loops straightened. Pedestrians walked without vanishing while traffic moved with steadier rhythm. The whole grid was pulling itself back into alignment.

Roe's voice was quiet but firm. "The system is responding."

Through the lab window they saw the park. A boy kicked

a football and it rolled in a clean arc then landed where it should. The children stared then burst into cheers.

Miriam let out a breath. "It's holding."

Across town, Professor March reached the end of his lecture. His chalk lines ran in order from first principle to final conclusion. Students clapped, more from relief than understanding. For the first time in weeks the class had begun and ended without the world breaking in between.

Nancy's cab swung round a junction. She gripped the wheel, ready for the lurch she had grown to dread. This time, the road held steady. She laughed aloud, startling her passenger. "At last. A corner that behaves itself."

Back in the lab, Roe adjusted the final dials. The glow softened and the vibrations eased. The last distortions on the display closed like cracks in cooling glass. The grid lay smooth. Left and right aligned with space once more and time ran forward in a single stream.

The machine powered down. Silence filled the lab broken only by the faint ticking of a wall clock. Its hands moved with calm precision.

Miriam leaned against the bench. "It's done."

Roe closed his notebook, the last page still marked with the evidence of what had been. "It's done," he agreed. "Straight lines again. But I'll never forget what we saw."

.~.

By evening the city had settled. Shops closed at their usual hours, buses rumbled through junctions without vanishing and families walked home from the park. Laughter rose from the playgrounds again. What had felt impossible hours before was now ordinary once more.

Roe walked with Miriam through the quiet streets. He kept his notebook tucked under one arm but did not open it. His gaze lingered on details others overlooked. The world was stable yet small reminders remained.

They passed a side road with a new sign. The paint was fresh, the letters crisp: *Yesterday Lane*. A name chosen by chance perhaps but Roe slowed as he read it. He knew what it marked. Not the past itself but the memory of what had almost taken root here.

The clock tower ticked above them in the square. Its chimes were steady but Roe noticed a subtle hitch in the sweep of the second hand like a faint pause before it moved on. Nobody else looked twice yet he could not unsee it.

"Still watching?" Miriam asked.

"I can't help it," Roe replied. "Everything seems fixed but you notice what's left behind."

She gave him a sidelong look. "The city's breathing again. People are safe. That's what matters."

They sat together on a bench near the fountain. Children splashed at the edge, throwing water at one another. Their shouts rose above the rush of traffic. Life was carrying on.

Roe opened his notebook at last. The pages were full of measurements with each mark tied to a moment of confusion and fear. He turned slowly until he reached the end. The final sketch remained as he had left it, a clear record of the displacement grid. He closed the book gently, humbled by the thought of what it represented.

"Will you keep it?" Miriam asked.

"Yes," Roe said. "To remind myself. Equations are not toys. They touch the world when you let them."

She nodded. "Then let it remind you and nothing more."

They rose and walked on. Past the shops, past the clock and past the street sign that hinted at what had almost come undone. For most, the day would be remembered only as a strange inconvenience. For Roe, it would remain as proof that time and space could be turned against themselves and that putting them back carried a cost no chalkboard could show.

3. THE STREETS OF ELSEWHEN

Physics suggests our universe may hold more than the three spatial dimensions we experience. Theories in high-energy physics describe additional dimensions, usually thought to be curled up at scales far smaller than atoms. There is nothing in our known physics, or even in so-called grand unified theories, to stop these extra dimensions growing large enough to be perceived in the real world.

What if extra dimensions swelled large enough to intersect with our own? What would they do to the human mind forced to walk them?

.~.

I walked into the district with map sheets tucked under my arm, neat and folded, the last crisp things I had. According to them this should have been simple. One straight road and two junctions. Nothing to trouble me.

But the air thickened as soon as I stepped past the corner. It clung to my skin, heavy, syrup-slow and every breath felt like it was pushing against water. My boots scuffed on pavement that lengthened beneath me. A kerb slid half a metre away while my foot still rested on it so I had to step twice just to keep balance.

Lampposts leaned as though ashamed of standing upright. When I blinked they snapped back then drooped again. Bricks on one side softened, edges smearing then hardened suddenly with mortar lines too sharp, too new, like the wall had rebuilt itself in an instant.

I opened my compass. The needle spun and wheeled wildly. For a moment it pointed north then veered inward. Dragging through me and tugging somewhere behind my breastbone. I slammed it shut but the tugging stayed, a phantom pull along ribs I didn't own.

I whispered numbers under my breath, a trick I used on long surveys to keep distance steady: *four paces, five, six...* but each count slipped. Four became eight then folded back to three. My voice doubled in my ears with an echo arriving before my lips moved.

The map in my hand seemed laughable. Fragile lines pretending to tame what writhed around me. I pressed my pencil hard, determined to fix one corner. I knew where it was, could feel the angle ready beneath the page. The moment the lead touched paper, the corner shuffled sideways, coy, mocking. The line landed crooked, already wrong.

My arm felt strange. I watched my sleeve wrinkle as I lifted it but the limb beneath was out of step, bending at a hinge halfway up the forearm that didn't exist. For a second my hand didn't belong to me. It was a stranger's fingers scribbling not quite following my thought.

The world kept twitching. A door slammed shut two houses ahead, echoing back before the sound could reach me. A man crossed the street twice, once with his scarf loose, once with it already tied. I blinked hard. For a flicker I saw myself already ahead, hunched, scribbling, my line darker, older. She turned. I turned. Both of me staring at both of us. My stomach lurched, bile rising.

I dropped the pencil.

The sound it made was sharp and cruel. The alley flinched around me with the walls stiffening. One line on the page pinned the street down, locking it into a single, dull geometry. The other possibilities quivered then whined like frightened dogs and folded themselves out of sight.

I pressed my palms to my eyes, trying to squeeze stillness into the world. But even in the dark the distortions wouldn't stop. Angles wriggled behind the lids. Shadows bulged like lungs. My own pulse felt doubled, staggered.

I lowered my hands once the street had stilled, or pretended to. A single road, narrow, simple. Nothing unusual at all. But I could feel the others beating beneath it like blood under skin that was waiting for me to slip again.

I told myself I was still Elara Quinn, cartographer, trained, rational. I had tools. I had methods. But my name sounded far away and the tools felt like toys pressed into a child's hand.

.~.

I tried to steady myself. A straight line, I told my feet. Just walk straight. But the pavement warped with every step, stretching long then snapping short. I had to lurch forward to keep from falling. My legs weren't mine or not entirely. Knees bent too early or too late or twice in the same stride.

The buildings leaned in close, whispering. Their windows rattled in a wind that wasn't blowing. A drainpipe shivered like a tuning fork. The sound burrowed into my jaw and fizzed at my teeth.

I touched my notebook and hoped the familiar weight would anchor me. The leather felt slick and damp as though I'd pulled it from a river. My fingers slipped, smearing across it. When I looked down, the page wasn't blank. It was already covered. Lines spidered across in my neat and practised handwriting but I hadn't drawn them. They bent into corners that didn't exist with alleys folding through one another. Some lines doubled back into spirals, some vanished into the paper as though falling through. I shut the book fast as my heart thudded.

My compass throbbed against my ribs. I pulled it out again. The needle jittered, spun then pointed not outwards but inward down through me. I could feel it tugging my chest hollow like there was a corridor inside. Some direction I'd never known my body contained. The pull made me nauseous like seasickness without the sea.

I pressed my free hand against the wall. Stone met me, rough and damp, but also not stone. My fingers sank a little like clay softening in the heat. Then something pulsed beneath, cool and alive, as though I was touching muscle under skin. My stomach clenched. I yanked back but a phantom palm still tingled there trapped in the wall.

The air grew heavy. Breathing turned to work. Each inhale was syrup, thick and sweet, coating my throat. Each exhale rattled, as though the street itself was breathing with me, keeping pace, forcing rhythm. I thought of lungs opening and closing around me, invisible, vast.

Colours began to bleed. The grey of the pavement seeped into my mouth, metallic and bitter. The sky pressed down a thin wash of blue that dripped cold through my throat. A smear of red graffiti on a wall buzzed against my teeth, hot and electric. I spat, but the taste stayed.

I stumbled dizzily and the world tilted. For a moment the ground was above me with the rooftops spread beneath. My arms windmilled with too many joints and bending wrong. My shoulder folded forward like a hinge then snapped back into place with a jolt of pain. I gasped clutching myself but my hands wouldn't line up, left tangled with right, fingers doubled and sliding.

I closed my eyes, praying for dark but dark was no refuge. Behind my lids staircases climbed into yellow skies that tasted of lemon and metal. Ladders slithered sideways into a purple haze with rung after rung melting like wax. Rooms unfolded like cardboard boxes turned inside-out and their walls fluttered like paper wings. Corners bent until they were planes. Planes collapsed until they were points and each point pulsed like a tiny star, breathing light into me. I couldn't tell if I was seeing or remembering or inventing. Or if those words even meant different things anymore.

A voice whispered in my ear but when I turned there was no one. The voice was inside my skull, echoing from bone. It said nothing clear. Only syllables turned liquid, melting into one

.~.

At first I thought I was dizzy. I stopped and pressed my palm to the wall. The bricks pulsed against me, warm, like muscle. My head dropped forward. When I looked up again there was someone ahead of me.

I froze.

She wore my coat. My satchel. My boots. She hunched just like me, hair falling across her glasses. In her hand, the notebook. My notebook. The pencil scratched, leaving marks before the tip touched down.

My throat clamped.

It should have been a reflection but the angle was wrong. No window, no mirror, no water. She was simply there, a few paces on.

Her head lifted. My head lifted. Our eyes met. The street dropped out from under me.

I split. One heartbeat here, the next half a pace ahead. Two sets of lungs, uneven. Fingers blurring into four hands, one clutching the strap, one scribbling furiously. My other self steadied while I staggered. Or I steadied while she staggered. We weren't one. We weren't two. We were a smear of butter spread thin across too much bread.

The world fractured.

I closed my eyes and hoped darkness would hold me steady. Instead it broke open. Staircases climbed upward into yellow skies that tasted sharp and metallic. Ladders slipped sideways into purple haze, rung after rung softening to wax beneath my feet. Rooms unfolded like boxes turned inside-out, their insides spread across me. Corners collapsed into planes, planes folded to points, and the points throbbed like stars, pulsing inside my skull. I wasn't sure if I was seeing or remembering or inventing. The words slipped apart until they were the same.

Language deserted me. *I— I can't— I—*

I doubled forward then doubled back. My mouth opened and three voices spilling out. One sobbing, one laughing, one whispering. My stomach heaved and bile burned. For a moment I was sure I would vomit myself onto the cobbles with both Elaras tangled in sick.

Then—snap.

A recoil like a rubber band let go.

I dropped to my knees. The notebook had fallen open and a single line ran across the page, black and steady. I stared at it, chest heaving. The line looked confident and certain but I hadn't meant to draw it. I didn't even remember the pencil touching.

And the street around me, the one outside the paper, had aligned with it. Straight, ordinary, cruelly fixed. All the other shivering possibilities I'd glimpsed just seconds before were gone.

I picked up the notebook with shaking fingers. My hand hovered over the page. For an instant I wanted to rip it and to tear the certainty apart. But the thought of what might spill loose if I did froze me in place.

I whispered, barely sound: *Stop drawing. Just stop.*

The words tasted hollow. The street held steady pinned by the line. Somewhere under my ribs the echo of the others still beat. The Elara I had been, the Elara I might be, the streets that had almost lived.

.~.

I kept drawing. I don't remember deciding to, but the pencil was already in my hand, dragging across paper. Each line came faster and harsher.

29

The street around me shimmered like water over stone. For a moment there were a dozen branches, alleyways bending away, flickering, crowding my vision. Some curved upward into pale light while others fell into shadow. They quivered like animals unsure of me.

I drew one. Just one. The line bit into the page.

The air locked. All the shimmering choices froze then blinked out leaving a single hard corner, dull and flat, ordinary as concrete. The weight of it crushed my chest.

I gasped, lifted the pencil then tried another. Again possibilities flinched, whimpered then folded away. Each stroke of graphite slammed the world into one shape and all the others shrank like dying things.

I stopped breathing. My mouth was dry and bitter. I hadn't meant harm. I only wanted to record and to steady. But the notebook had teeth.

The thought lodged sharp in my head. Mapping wasn't harmless. Mapping was murder.

The streets didn't vanish quietly. They curled at the edges, tugging, begging. For every line I fixed, there was a sigh, a cry, a tug at my ribs as if a limb were being torn off. I pressed my hand against my chest, dizzy with loss that wasn't mine, or maybe it was.

I tried to steady myself, rationalise. Cartographers don't kill. Lines on paper don't bleed. But the pavement under my boots said otherwise. Each mark I made echoed through the stones, flattening them into dull obedience.

I looked at the page. The drawing was ugly and scrawled yet the street obeyed it, matching every slip of my hand. If I trembled, the world trembled. If I forced a line straight then the world bent back into that straightness.

I wanted to stop. I wanted to fling the notebook into the gutter and let the streets breathe again. But the habit was too strong. The compulsion of training, of years drawing maps, measuring, recording. I had been raised to fix things in place.

Now I knew the cost.

I set the pencil down slowly, afraid of even that movement. The silence after was thick. Around me, the street was plain, rigid, stripped of shimmer. No voices, no doubling, no choices. Only one road.

I stared at the paper with the thin black lines and the neat angles. It looked like control but all I could see was absence. A map of what I had killed.

.~.

I can't tell when the street ended. Or if it did. Corners slid into one another, bending, folding, until the ground was less a road than a swirl of directions stacked on top of me. I tried to walk but each step landed heavy and slow as if air itself had turned to treacle.

My thoughts dragged. Each one started clean then sagged sideways before it could finish. A number, a measurement, gone before I could hold it. The pencil felt soft in my hand, melting and stretching like warm wax.

Walls pulsed. They weren't walls anymore. They were lungs, or hearts, beating. The sound reached me thickly inside my skull like I was the one panting. I pressed my palm against the nearest surface. It shivered under me then sucked at my hand like wet clay, trying to take me in.

I pulled back too slow, toffee-slow and for a moment I thought part of me had stayed behind. My chest hurt with a hollow beat out of rhythm with the rest of me.

The air tasted wrong. Blue slid down my throat, cold and metallic. Yellow pressed bitter on my tongue. Red rattled in my teeth until I clenched my jaw against it. I coughed and colours sprayed in the dark like paint thrown against glass.

My body bent strange. My arm had more joints than it should. My legs didn't meet where they once had. I stumbled but the stumble took minutes, maybe hours. I was still falling, still standing, both, neither.

Voices hummed in my head. Not words, just echoes of words

that never finished. They looped then started again then curled inside one another. I tried to answer, to tell them to stop but my mouth opened slowly, too slowly and no sound left me.

I saw stairs climbing nowhere, turning into colour at the top. Doorways opened inside-out, handles on the wrong side, hinges beating like wings. Light pooled thick as milk, folding across itself, shining from behind me, inside me, everywhere.

I thought: *I'm breaking.*

The thought didn't stick. It slid away.

I tried again: *I'm...* and then it dissolved.

The pencil dropped. It floated down, slow, slower, the scrape of graphite against paper stretched into a sound longer than breath. The line it left curved into nothing then into everything. For an instant the street convulsed, flinched and cried out. Or maybe it was me crying out.

I pressed my face into my hands but even the dark wouldn't hold. Angles wriggled in the black, crawling. My heartbeat staggered. I wasn't sure which ribs belonged to me anymore.

When I lowered my hands the world hadn't reformed. It swam. Heavy, sweet and suffocating.

I thought if I stayed I would dissolve too.

.~.

I sat on the kerb, though it didn't feel like sitting. The stones slid under me then melted and reset. My body was heavy, too heavy, sinking through my own bones.

The notebook lay open on my lap with its pages rippling like water. Lines I didn't remember drawing sprawled across them. Alleys, corners, whole districts etched in graphite. Some bent inward, some outward, some not at all. They looked alive, twitching, squirming, like worms caught in light.

I lifted the pencil. Or it lifted me. My arm rose syrup-slow, elbow bending in three places instead of one. The air thickened around the tip, pulling it down, pulling me down. The street around me quivered, waiting, as if hungry for the mark.

I wanted to let it fall. To press the lead, fix another path and quiet the shiver of possibilities. One stroke and everything would lock again. Safe. Ordinary.

But my chest ached. Not from fear but from the weight of what I'd already done. I could feel them, the alleys I had killed, whispering under my skin. They didn't hate me. They mourned me.

My hand trembled. The pencil wavered above the paper, casting a shadow longer than it should. I felt the air lean in, begging.

"No," I whispered, voice dry. My lips cracked with the word.

The air pushed harder. My hand buckled. The page swelled beneath the pencil point, eager.

"No." Louder this time.

I dropped the pencil. It clattered sharp against the kerb, the only sound that rang clean. The street flinched. The notebook stilled.

For a long moment I sat there, panting, eyes fixed on the blank space where the pencil had nearly touched. Slowly, like a fog lifting, a thought returned to me.

Maybe if I stop, it stops too.

The idea was fragile, uncertain but it was mine. My own. I repeated it, holding it tight, tasting the words until they steadied.

The streets shivered once more as though disappointed. Then they quieted. Around me, the world aligned into one simple road, narrow and plain. I knew it wasn't the whole truth. The other paths still pulsed, waiting, hidden just beyond sight in another dimension. But for now they stayed there and I stayed here.

I picked up the notebook with steadier hands. I closed it. The cover thudded shut, final, ordinary.

For the first time in hours or years or whatever this had been, I felt something close to solid ground beneath me. Not safe, not certain but bearable.

I breathed, slow and even.

I would not draw again.

.~.

I am steadier now, steadier than I was. The syrup has thinned. The air no longer claws at me. My hands are my own again even if the skin still hums with memory.

I know, at last, what I've been walking through. Not madness. Not dream. Something deeper.

The world is not four. Not three plus one. There are others. Directions hidden in the fold of things. Angles that don't belong to our box of space and time. I touched them. They touched me. The streets were only where they spilled through, like cracks in plaster showing the beams beneath.

Every time I tried to draw, I nailed one beam into place. One dimension showing itself, mundane and obedient. The rest recoiled. Not gone but only withdrawn and waiting. My maps didn't record. They forced. Each line collapsed the swell of possibilities into one single surface.

That's why the walls breathed, why colours bled into taste, why I doubled inside myself. My body was straining into shapes it doesn't have names for. The compass spinning in my ribs, the phantom joints, the voices before words. All echoes from those other angles pressing against me.

I killed them. Not the whole of them, you can't kill dimensions, but I silenced the glimpses. Fixed them flat. Reduced them to one street, one corner, one everyday geometry.

I shut the notebook. I let it rest and, when I stopped drawing, the pressure eased. The city held steady or pretended to. One road. One moment.

But I still feel the tug. Behind me, beneath me, inside me. The streets are not gone. They are elsewhere. Elsewhen. Pressing soft against the skin of things, waiting for the next crack.

I walk back slowly, holding the notebook closed. I don't dare open it again. I know now what the pages can do.

Some paths are not meant to be mapped. Some corners must stay unfixed or the world risks losing what lies beyond.

But still I wonder, if I let myself linger, would they pull me through? Would I step off the pavement and find myself in the other dimensions, body unwound, thought stretched sideways, never to return?

The answer waits just beyond sight. Beating, breathing. Patient.

4. SHORT MEASURES

Measurement is the quiet backbone of science. A metre today is the same as a metre tomorrow. Two rods joined end to end must always add up to their combined length. This trust in additivity underpins everything: engineering, navigation, architecture, even the certainty that a wall will meet at its corners. Without it, the world itself would not hold together.

But what if that rule was not fixed? What if space itself refused to obey the simple arithmetic we take for granted?

.~.

T he call came at dawn. I drove through the mist with a weight in my chest that felt like memory rather than expectation. They said an object had fallen and I was needed.

At the site I found the ground scorched but not broken. No crater, no debris. Instead a smooth black sphere hovered within a faint blue haze. It was no larger than a medicine ball yet it carried a presence that made the air tighten. On its surface a red hexagon glowed sharp against the black. Beside it shimmered the words *Don't Press*, written in shifting scripts that I recognised and others I didn't.

I circled the dome they had built around it. Instruments

lined the perimeter. Radiation monitors and field sensors and magnetometers. All showed nothing unusual. Yet the sphere hummed faintly with a vibration I could feel more than hear.

I pulled out my notebook. I prefer paper for first impressions. A clean page, the date, the conditions and a sketch of the object. The act steadied me. I measured distance with careful steps, noting each change in light and sound.

The sphere seemed to respond. When I leaned close the haze pulsed brighter. When I stepped back it dimmed. I tested this several times, slow and precise. The pattern held.

I wrote one sentence in the margin: *It is aware.*

That thought chilled me more than I cared to admit. I closed the notebook but the pressure in the room did not ease. The red hexagon glowed as though it had been waiting for me in particular.

The team asked if it could be moved. I hesitated. Every instinct warned me to keep it undisturbed. Yet the longer it remained in the field, the more curious eyes would gather. I agreed but insisted on complete control of the procedure.

A containment cradle was built then lined with dampers and sensors. The sphere settled onto it without resistance though the haze thickened when metal touched its surface. I walked beside the rig as it was wheeled into the transport bay. The hum followed us.

The journey to the laboratory was short. We sealed the object in a reinforced chamber set within a climate-controlled vault. I checked each monitor myself: temperature, field strength, vibration, radiation. All read normal. Yet nothing about it felt normal.

I stood alone for a moment after the others had left. The sphere hovered in its cradle, red hexagon glowing, haze pulsing like breath. My hand tightened around the notebook. The words on its surface seemed to shift once more.

Don't Press.

It felt less like a warning and more like a challenge.

The laboratory was quiet that evening. I had dismissed the technicians after the final round of checks. Too many eyes bred too much impatience and this object deserved patience above all.

I sat at the console with my notebook open. My sketches of the sphere were scattered with annotations, each one more tentative than the last. Radiation, magnetic field, temperature, pressure. All stable. No emission beyond the faint hum that tickled the air and crawled into the bones.

The red hexagon glowed steadily, neither bright nor dim, as if waiting for me to exhaust every measurement. *Don't Press.* The words shimmered faintly beside it, in English, Russian, Mandarin, Arabic. Every time I looked they shifted order but the meaning was never lost.

I tested its reactions again. A hand brought close made the haze pulse. A pen tapped against the cradle frame caused the hum to rise by a fraction of a tone. I logged everything down to the second. My pencil pressed hard into the paper until the tip broke.

I sat back with heavy heart. For years I had taught my students that the role of the experimentalist was restraint. To measure carefully. To record without prejudice. To let the universe speak first. Yet here it seemed the universe had delivered an ultimatum. Nothing would change until I pressed that mark.

I tried to reason with myself. What if it triggered an explosion? What if something came out the sphere? What if the effect spread beyond the walls? What if pressing was not an act of science at all but of arrogance? My mind listed each danger with crisp clarity yet none removed the simple fact that discovery required contact.

I rose and approached the cradle. The sphere hung silent and steady. My hand hovered above the red glow. I whispered aloud what I could not bear to leave unspoken. "Curiosity has always been the risk."

I pressed.

At first nothing. Then the air seemed to tighten as though the room had been pulled taut. I staggered back, blinking at the bench. Something was wrong. The edge of the tabletop no longer met the cabinet cleanly. A faint gap had opened, small but undeniable.

I crouched and looked at the tiles near my feet. Their neat grid looked distorted as if a fraction of each had gone missing. The effect was subtle, enough to doubt my own eyes, yet it set my heart racing.

I turned to the bench where my measuring rods lay. If anything was amiss then the numbers would show it. I laid two tens end to end and drew the tape across them.

Eighteen.

The numbers were impossible yet consistent. Space itself had bent, not in collapse but in arithmetic.

I wrote a single word in my notebook, the letters jagged with the tremor in my hand: *Changed.*

.~.

The sphere remained still, as if nothing had happened but the world around it had shifted. I knew at once this was no illusion. I reached for a second ruler. Ten added to ten again gave eighteen. Twenty beside thirty gave forty. Each sum was short of what it should be.

I repeated the tests with callipers, tape measures, laser rangefinders. All told the same story. Lengths were absolute in isolation. A rod was still exactly twenty centimetres. A block still thirty. Yet when I combined them, the totals failed. Not random, not unstable, but altered with perfect consistency.

I felt the weight of the discovery pressing on me. This was not noise in the data, not a mis-calibration. The rule itself had shifted. The universe inside this chamber no longer obeyed addition.

I marked out a grid on the floor, measuring tile against tile. The effect held. Each step was true on its own, but three steps together did not match the expected sum. I scribbled diagrams, cross-checking, repeating, confirming. My hand ached but I dared not stop until I had mapped the pattern.

The boundary was clear. At first it hugged the cradle, no more than a metre across. Beyond that line, addition worked as it always had. Inside, the anomaly ruled. I tested the edge by sliding a rod slowly across it, half in, half out. One end measured true. The other obeyed the new arithmetic. The join between them was abrupt, like crossing into another geometry.

I asked the technicians to stand back. None of them argued. They sensed the strangeness as well. I closed the chamber doors, set the locks and made certain the readings outside remained ordinary. They did. For now, the anomaly was confined.

But even as I checked, I felt a slow creep. Two metres today, perhaps more tomorrow. The field was spreading. If it reached beyond the laboratory walls, containment would fail.

I leaned on the bench and my pencil paused above the page. I wrote: *Additivity broken. Expansion steady. Urgency rising.*

For the first time in my life, I was afraid not of what I had found but of what might happen if I did nothing.

.~.

By the third day the field had reached the annex where a group of contractors were fitting a new research wing. I had told myself the anomaly could be managed quietly inside the laboratory, but I was wrong.

I found two builders staring at the north wall. Their tape measure read true on each section yet the final gap refused to close. The bricks overlapped by a hand's breadth when they forced them together and if they aligned one end the other sagged open. The foreman cursed his crew and accused them of sloppy work.

I asked them to stop and fetched a laser line. Over a single span the measurement was perfect, but the same run broken into smaller sections came up short. I kept my thoughts to myself. "Use uniform cuts," I told them. "One size, repeat it. Don't mix lengths." They looked puzzled but obeyed. The wall settled more neatly on the second attempt. I wrote a quiet note in my book: *Additive failure confirmed outside chamber.*

On the fourth day the plumbing crew called me. A run of pipes refused to land on its mountings. Two lengths of metal and a connector measured correctly apart but together they stopped short of the target by several centimetres. I ordered a flexible length installed instead in one continuous span. The pipe fitted first time. The crew muttered about warped fittings but I said nothing.

The same pattern repeated with wiring harnesses. Segments cut to different lengths twisted against each other and refused to reach their boxes. I walked the corridors with a pocket notebook, issuing instructions, keeping the complaints contained. I blamed faulty tools, poor calibration, anything that sounded mundane. Behind the excuses my heart was sinking. The anomaly had grown beyond theory. It was now undermining the work of ordinary people who had no idea what they were facing.

Each evening I returned to the sphere. It hovered in its cradle with the red hexagon steady and the haze pulsing like breath. The field expanded in all directions from the sphere by two metres a day. I checked the edge with rods laid end to end and marked the line where the arithmetic failed. On day four it reached the annex wall eight metres from the cradle. By day ten it spilled into the service corridor at fourteen metres. The inner fence stood another thirty metres beyond, so I had less than three weeks before the boundary touched it.

Containment was slipping through my fingers. If the anomaly breached the outer compound, it would touch the town within days. Builders would not stay quiet then. Roads would not close, houses would not stand. The truth would break free.

I closed the chamber doors and leaned against the cool metal. My hand shook as I wrote the final line for the day: *Expansion steady. Control diminishing.*

The warning on the sphere burned in my mind. *Don't Press.* Yet each passing hour whispered that pressing it again might be the only way to stop the creep before the world noticed.

I told myself I still had time but the notebook in my hand felt heavier than ever as if the decision had already been made.

.~.

I stayed late that night. The others had gone home, leaving the corridors empty and the hum of the ventilation as my only companion. I pulled a set of rods onto the bench—10, 20, 25, 30 centimetres—and laid my notebook open beside them. If there was a rule, it had to show itself in these numbers.

I began with the obvious. Ten plus ten. I aligned the rods, marked the total, and checked it against a fresh measure. Eighteen. Again, and again, the same. Consistent. I underlined it twice in my notes.

I added a third rod of ten. The total should have been thirty, yet the join gave me twenty-seven. I added a fourth, and the sum became thirty-six instead of forty. The percentage was unchanged. Still ten per cent short no matter how many rods I combined, so long as they were all the same length.

That steadied me. It told me the loss was not about quantity, but about variety. The lengths themselves carried the rule.

I moved to the twenties. Two rods gave me thirty-six instead of forty. Three rods gave fifty-four instead of sixty. The same ten per cent reduction, consistent across the board.

Then I changed the set. Twenty plus thirty. The total should have been fifty, yet it measured forty. A full twenty per cent loss. My pulse quickened.

I tried twenty plus twenty-five. The expected forty-five shrank to thirty-six. Again twenty per cent.

I pushed further. Twenty plus twenty-five plus thirty. The true sum was seventy-five. The measure came to fifty-two and a half. Thirty per cent short.

I sat back, staring at the numbers. My pencil tapped hard against the page, leaving dents in the paper. The pattern was emerging but I forced myself to test again. Different orders, different groupings.

Twenty plus twenty-five first gave me thirty-six, then added to thirty gave sixty. But if I joined all three in one operation, the result was fifty-two and a half.

It was systematic. One distinct length meant a ten per cent loss. Two different lengths meant twenty. Three meant thirty. The more variety, the greater the penalty. And worse, the grouping mattered. Add them step by step and the total shifted. Non-associative. The outcome depended on the path you took.

The figures blurred on the page as my eyes watered. It was not despair. It was exhilaration. For hours I had been drowning in contradictions but here at last was a law. A law as strict as any in physics though it belonged to a geometry I had never imagined.

I wrote in capital letters: *LOSS = 10% × NUMBER OF DISTINCT LENGTHS.*

I laughed, a short and ragged sound in the silent room. Eureka, though I did not say the word aloud. I had been broken open by it, as much as Archimedes had been in his bath.

Newton padded into the lab with his tail flicking and leapt onto the bench. He blinked at me, indifferent, as though alien geometry was of no concern to him. I scratched behind his ears with shaking fingers.

"It makes sense," I whispered. "God help me, but it makes sense."

.~.

The answer gave me no peace. If anything it pressed harder against my thoughts, a weight I could not put down. The law was precise and merciless. Ten per cent lost for each distinct length. A geometry that mocked the certainty I had built my career upon.

I closed the notebook and set the pencil aside. My eyes turned to the sphere. It floated in its cradle and the red hexagon pulsed faintly as though it had been listening. I thought of the builders, the pipes and the harnesses. All those quiet fixes, each one a lie to buy a little more time. The field was still growing and soon no trick would hide it.

I rose slowly. My hand brushed the page one last time, smudging the ink of the law I had written. I walked to the chamber, unlocked the heavy doors and stood before the sphere.

The warning shimmered as it always had. *Don't Press.* The words hung in a dozen languages, changing order as my eyes moved. It was no longer a prohibition. It was a challenge.

I placed my palm above the hexagon and felt the hum climb into my bones. My heart pounded. Rational thought screamed restraint. Yet the other voice, the one that had carried me through years of experiment, whispered back: discovery always costs.

I pressed.

For a moment, nothing. Then the room split open. The laboratory dissolved into three overlapping visions, each one clear and undeniable.

In one, the geometry snapped back. Rulers added cleanly. Bricks met at their corners. Builders laughed with relief, unaware how close the world had come to bending beyond repair. The sphere lay inert, no more than a relic.

In another, the air shimmered with light. A doorway formed, quivering, translucent. Tall figures stepped through with deliberate grace. Their eyes moved across the room, calculating, understanding. They looked at me not as a man out of his depth but as a student who had answered enough to be called forward.

In the third, chaos. Floors stretched and folded. Walls warped like wet paper. The past bled through the present in jagged flashes. I saw birds frozen mid-flight outside the window, seasons clashing against one another in a flickering storm. The exhilaration and terror struck like lightning.

All three pressed against me at once. I felt myself swaying, my mind split in three directions. Observation had always chosen outcomes, but this time the choice was mine alone.

I closed my eyes. I slowed my breathing. Steady hands. Calm mind. Patience. Then I reached inward, willing the one path into being.

When I opened my eyes, the shimmer remained. The figures were waiting.

.~.

I raised my hand, not to press again, but to signal assent. The chaos and the false restoration thinned like fog before sunlight. The laboratory stabilised. The figures remained.

I tried to write but my pen shook too much to form words. Newton leapt onto the bench beside me and curled himself into a ball, purring as though nothing in the universe had shifted. I envied him his constancy.

The tallest figure leaned forward. Not a voice but a current of meaning pressed into my thoughts. *You pressed. You observed. You understood.*

I felt awe and fear in equal measure. "And now?" I asked, though my lips barely moved.

The answer came without sound: *Now, we decide.*

The weight of that judgement filled the room. It was no longer my experiment alone. It was humanity's trial and the outcome would not rest in my hands alone.

I looked down at Newton then back at the figures. "Then tell us," I whispered. "Show us what comes next."

The shimmer deepened and the universe seemed to lean closer.

Their presence was quiet but immense. Meaning pressed into me like a tide, vast and unstoppable. They did not speak yet my mind filled with images. Cities folded and refolded as if walls were pages in a book. Stars bent into shapes beyond geometry, spirals within spirals, each carrying a rhythm of its own. Bridges of light reached between worlds, shrinking and stretching with no loss, no fracture.

It was less explanation than demonstration yet the message was clear. The hexagon had never been ours. It was a test, a doorway, a glimpse into rules we had mistaken for absolutes.

The doorway pulsed behind them. Not merely with possibility but with intent. This was not only conversation. It was inspection, judgement, decision. Humanity's curiosity had opened the path but our readiness to walk it remained in question.

I clutched my notebook though the pen trembled too much to write. Newton purred softly at my side, grounding me in the present while the universe tilted toward futures I could barely comprehend.

The tallest figure leaned closer. Their eyes met mine, unreadable, infinite. The thought that reached me was both invitation and warning.

You pressed. You observed. You understood. Now, we decide.

And in that silence, I realised that reality itself might bend again.

5. TROUBLE WITH TACHYONS

Tachyons are a hypothetical class of particles that would always move faster than light. Unlike ordinary matter, they would not slow down if energy were taken away. Instead, they would accelerate, rushing ever faster the less they were given. To bring them down to light speed would demand an infinite amount of energy, an impossible task. Their equations also predict an imaginary mass, a feature that makes them seem more like mathematical phantoms than real particles.

But what if they were real? What if a device could call them into service? Forcing them, just for an instant, to carry information backwards through time or spill echoes of other possibilities into our world.

.~.

The museum at night was never really silent. Its floors creaked and its pipes hummed and sometimes the stuffed owl above the entrance looked ready to swoop. I should have been frightened, locked in after hours, but I wasn't. I felt as though the place had been handed over to me with every exhibit mine to wander through.

I was halfway across the great hall when I heard it. A

sudden whoop of joy, muffled through walls but so sharp and unexpected it made me stop dead. No one should have been here. Yet the sound had come from the closed-off observatory wing, the one the museum brochures never mentioned.

Curiosity prickled stronger than fear. I padded closer. A thin seam of light spilled under the door, pulsing faintly as if in rhythm with a heartbeat. I hesitated then pushed it open a crack.

Inside stood a woman I had never seen before. Her dark hair was tied in a messy braid, her lab coat half unbuttoned. She hovered over a workbench crowded with wires, glass tubes and coils that glowed faintly as though alive. At the centre sat a screen with green letters marching across it in bright, impossible words:

HELLO ELENA. MESSAGE RECEIVED.

The woman clapped her hands once, a laugh bubbling out of her. She spun in a half-circle then saw me in the doorway and froze.

"Oh!" she exclaimed. Then, instead of anger, her face broke into a grin. "Did you hear that? It worked!"

I blinked. "You... you're not staff here, are you?"

"Not officially," she admitted, brushing a stray wire from her sleeve. "I borrow the space when it's quiet. I'm Elena."

I hugged my book closer. "Tamsin."

"Well, Tamsin, you've arrived at the perfect moment." She gestured wildly at the machine. "It's never done this before!"

I stepped inside, caught by the thrill in her voice. "What is it?"

"A communication rig," she said, still slightly breathless. "I've been working on it for months and just now it finally sent a message back to me."

I frowned. "Back?"

"Back in time," she corrected, eyes shining. She tapped the screen. "Look, the machine predicted this greeting before I even typed it."

I stared. Another line appeared as though answering us:

TIME OFFSET: MINUS TWELVE SECONDS.

"Watch carefully," she said. Her fingers darted over the keyboard, spelling out a new line. But before she finished, the words *ARE YOU WATCHING?* had already appeared at the top of the screen.

I gasped. "It showed it first!"

"Yes!" Elena cried, bouncing on her toes like a girl half her age. "Do you see? The signal outruns light itself. Tachyons are particles faster than light. They nudge information into the past."

Her excitement was infectious. I felt my chest fizz with it.

Before I knew what I was doing, I reached toward a smaller console attached to the main device. A blue button pulsed beneath my finger. Elena opened her mouth, maybe to warn me, but I pressed it anyway. I've always been a bit impulsive.

Across the bench, a second screen flickered into life.

HELLO FROM THE OTHER SIDE.

The keyboard beneath my hand rattled a heartbeat later, catching up as if I had already decided what to write.

For a moment the room felt impossibly wide as though time itself had bent open.

Elena slapped the bench, half in disbelief, half in delight. "Yes! Oh, Tamsin, you've done it again. It's working! You've just sent your first tachyon message!"

I could only stare at the glowing letters. I hadn't meant to but I'd spoken to the future and the future had spoken back.

.~.

Elena leaned back against the bench, breathing fast. Her grin hadn't faded though the machine's screen was already dimming and the green letters flickered like tired fireflies.

"Is it supposed to fade like that?" I asked.

"Supposed to?" She laughed. "There isn't a 'supposed to.'

Nothing like this has ever worked before tonight. I've been building it for months, chasing equations most people dismissed as nonsense. I thought it would take another year at least to coax anything out of it." She shook her head, braid swishing. "But here it is. Talking back."

Her voice had that same buzz I felt in my chest: half fear and half wonder.

"Why here?" I asked. "Why the museum?"

"The university wouldn't touch me," she admitted. "Too risky, too strange. The museum had space no one cared about and a few old coils and mirrors I could salvage. I made a deal with the curator. He gets a free lecture when I'm ready and I get silence to work in until then." She gave me a sly smile. "Until you stumbled in."

I flushed but stood straighter. "You said it worked because I pressed the button."

"That's right. Maybe the machine needed a fresh set of hands. Or maybe it wanted an audience." She crouched beside the console, fiddling with wires. "Here, watch the dials. If they climb above the red line, tap them down."

I perched on the stool with heart thudding. The dials twitched like nervous eyes. One needle crept up brushing the red mark. I tapped it lightly and the machine's hum steadied.

"Good," Elena murmured. "Keep it there."

For a minute everything seemed fine. Then the screen spasmed with words smearing across it in tangled green scribbles. The hum rose to a shriek and sparks spat from one of the tubes.

"Elena!"

She darted forward and yanked a lever. The noise cut off leaving a ringing silence. Sharp and acrid smoke curled from the glass tube.

"Well," she said, coughing once, "that answers the question of whether the generator is stable."

I couldn't help laughing though my hands shook. "It's broken?"

"Not broken," she said peering at the tube. "Just overexcited. The tachyon field wobbled out of phase. Happens when you push it too far." She straightened and wiped her hands. "But even a wobble means it was real. That message, your message, wasn't an illusion."

I looked at the screen still faintly glowing. "*HELLO FROM THE OTHER SIDE*" lingered ghostlike and half-erased by static. My chest tightened. "That was me. I actually did that."

"Yes, you did." Elena smiled and it wasn't the grin of triumph she'd worn earlier but something softer. "That's why I'm glad you came. Science is never neat on the first try. It sparks, it smokes, it falls apart. But you saw through the mess to what matters."

I pressed my palm flat on the bench, grounding myself in the hum of it. "It's not magic is it?"

"No," she said firmly. "It only feels that way until you learn the rules. You want to know them?"

I nodded before I even thought about it.

"Then you'll have to help me test it when I rebuild. Machines break, Tamsin. But curiosity doesn't. That's what keeps us trying."

.~.

Elena wasn't the sort of person who gave up. By the time I came back the next evening, yes I sneaked out again, my nerves jangling the whole way, she already had the generator open with wires spilling across the bench like tangled roots. A fresh glass tube glowed faintly where the old one had cracked.

"Back again, Tamsin?" she said without looking up. Her voice was tired but cheerful. "Good. I need another pair of hands."

I dropped my bag by the door. "Is it safe?"

"Safe enough," she replied, tightening a screw. "Though we'll take it slowly. Machines like this don't forgive impatience."

She gave me a crooked grin.

The hum returned when she powered it up. Gentler this time. No words scrolled across the screen. Instead, she slid a shallow dish into place at the centre.

"We're not asking for messages tonight," she explained. "I want to see how the field behaves around simple matter."

From under the bench she produced a potted flower, its petals still closed tight against the evening chill. "Set it in the dish. Then nudge the lever forward. Just a little."

My hands trembled as I obeyed. The coils gave a faint whine. The petals stirred, twitched then spread in a slow spiral until the bloom was open and golden.

I gasped. "It bloomed, right here and now!"

Elena's eyes shone. "Hours of growth compressed into seconds. The tachyons have coupled with the molecular vibrations inside the cells. When they run slightly ahead, processes accelerate." She tapped the humming coil. "It's not random. It's resonance. Think of two pendulums pushing each other, faster and faster, until one drags the other forward."

I laughed, almost dizzy with it. "Can we try something else?"

She handed me a tumbler of ice. "Forward accelerates. Back slows. Your turn."

I set it in the dish and pushed the lever forward. The cubes shrank rapidly, mist clouding the glass as water trickled to the bottom.

"It's still cold," I said, touching it.

"Of course. The energy flows the same way, it just flows quicker. The ice isn't hotter but time itself is thinner here."

I shivered, not from cold. Then, carefully, I drew the lever back. The hum softened to a low purr. The drops of water hesitated on the cubes then trembled but refused to fall.

"It's like pressing pause," I whispered.

"Exactly," she said. "Everything slows when the tachyons slip out of step. Imagine trying to clap in rhythm to a song but lagging just behind. The music pulls you back. That's what the field does to matter." She leaned closer, voice dropping. "It's not magic, Tamsin. There are rules. Patterns you can learn even if they're not the ones in your schoolbooks."

Her words thrilled me more than the glowing machines. Rules meant it wasn't a trick. It was knowable and waiting to be mapped.

Elena must have seen the fire in my eyes because she stepped back and let me keep my hands on the controls. "Then you'll help me chart those patterns. We'll need patience. The generator will wobble again, no doubt. But, with care, we'll see how far the rules bend before they break."

I nodded fiercely. I didn't just want to watch. I wanted to understand.

.~.

By the third evening, I thought I knew what to expect. The hum of the coils, Elena's restless energy and another strange trial that bent the rules just enough to make my head spin. But that night she had something new waiting on the bench. A squat box with a circular screen and a row of jumpy dials.

"This one isn't polished," she warned while adjusting a loose wire. "It's a detector, tuned to tachyons that don't sit neatly in our world. If the generator holds steady it should let us see echoes."

"Echoes of what?" I asked, sliding onto the stool.

Her eyes gleamed. "Other arrangements of things. Perhaps other versions of here. But don't expect order. Tachyons don't like to be held."

She flicked the switch. The screen glowed grey, static buzzing faintly. At first it showed nothing. Then shapes surfaced, shelves, walls and doorways but shifted, wrong. The door was on the far wall and the shelves reversed.

"It's the museum," I whispered, "but not our museum."

Elena laughed under her breath. "Yes! Do you see? Tachyons

53

slip across boundaries. They give us a glimpse of other possibilities."

The image quivered. My stomach turned cold. A figure stood in the ghost-room. It was me, or someone like me! Shorter hair and a different jumper. She leaned over a notebook, writing furiously, lips moving as if reciting. Then the picture collapsed into noise.

"That was me," I said hoarsely.

"An echo," Elena breathed. "Another path you might have taken."

The dials twitched harder. The screen flared bright showing a hall lit by lanterns with people in clothes from another century. A squeal split the air and the box rattled on its feet.

"Elena!"

She darted forward and slammed a lever down. The glow died leaving the room in sudden silence. A curl of smoke rose from the box.

My heart hammered. "Magic smoke! That could have been nasty."

She pushed her braid back, eyes still alight. "It could have been. Tachyons are unruly by nature. Normal particles slow down when you drain their energy. Tachyons do the opposite. The less you give them, the faster they run."

I frowned. "Faster?"

"Yes. Try to slow them toward light speed and they resist with infinity. That's why the field slipped. The generator tried to leash them and they bolted. They don't want to be steady. They always want to outrun the leash."

I hugged my arms tight and stared at the blank screen. "So we can't really control them?"

"Not easily," she said, crouching beside the box. "We can guide them for a while but push too far and they drag the system into chaos. That's the trouble with tachyons. They're real enough to show us wonders but wild enough to tear through the walls if you let them."

Her tone should have warned me but instead it set fire to my thoughts. Wonders. Walls. Other versions of me. I wanted to see more even if it meant chaos.

Elena caught my expression and gave a wry smile. "Don't look so disappointed. Science is built on failure as much as success. Every wobble teaches us what the rules are. Knowing there are rules is what matters."

The smoke cleared but the faint smell of burning lingered. I knew I should have been afraid. Instead, all I could think of was the girl in the other museum bent over her notebook and what she might have been writing.

.~.

The smell of scorched wires clung to the air long after the detector had fallen silent. I kept staring at it, waiting for the screen to flicker back to life but it stayed dark. My heart hadn't slowed.

Elena leaned against the bench wiping her hands on a rag. "You see now why I called it trouble," she said. "Tachyons don't behave. The harder you try to slow them, the wilder they get. They rush faster and faster with less energy input as though they're laughing at us for trying to catch them."

I swallowed. "But we really saw those other places didn't we? That wasn't my imagination."

Her eyes softened. "No. They were genuine echoes. Fragments of other arrangements and other paths. We can't step into them, not with anything I can build here. But we can glimpse them. That's already more than most people will ever know."

I hugged my arms, the thrill still fizzing in my veins. "Why am I allowed to see this? I mean, shouldn't it be hidden? Dangerous?"

Elena tilted her head, studying me. "The universe doesn't choose who notices it, Tamsin. Most people walk past without looking. You looked. That's enough."

"But I don't understand any of it," I blurted. "I don't even know proper physics. I couldn't explain half of what I just saw."

She laughed softly. "Neither can I. Not fully. No one can. What matters is that you want to. That hunger is rarer than you think." She set the rag down, her expression serious now. "Curiosity is a gift but it's also heavy. If you follow it, it won't always be safe. There will be nights like this one when machines smoke and rules slip sideways. You'll have to decide if you want to walk that path."

I couldn't speak. The words felt too big in my throat.

She went on more gently, "I'm not asking for an answer tonight. But if you do want to follow that route then come back next summer. The museum runs student programmes. On paper you'll be a volunteer, shifting boxes and cataloguing slides, but you and I will know it's more than that. If you still care by then I'll show you what else tachyons can do."

Her gaze held mine, steady and certain.

I nodded, almost before I realised I was moving.

Later, when she walked me to the door, the night outside felt vast, the stars sharper than I'd ever seen them. My footsteps echoed all the way down the street, each one carrying the same thought. There are rules to this even if I don't know them yet. Rules that twist and shimmer but never break without reason.

It wasn't magic. It wasn't luck. It was something deeper, something waiting to be uncovered.

The trouble with tachyons was that they wouldn't stand still. But maybe that was also their gift. They pulled you forward, faster than you thought you could run until the path curved back on itself and carried you somewhere unexpected.

I think that was the moment I decided. Not out loud, not in words anyone else would notice. But a decision deep enough that it never left me. One day I would learn the rules. One day I would study physics and I would come back ready to understand the trouble with tachyons.

.~.

Years later, she would remember the museum nights not for the smoke or the broken tubes but for the feeling that the world had cracked open and shown a glimpse of something larger. The first message on the glowing screen, the flower blooming too soon, the frozen drip of water, the ghostly image of herself writing in another place. All of it lived sharper in her memory than any lesson from school. She hadn't had the words then, only the certainty that rules existed and could be learned. That certainty never left her. It was the spark that turned curiosity into purpose and purpose into a life's work.

6. TIMELIKE ECHOES

Closed timelike loops (CTLs) are a theoretical feature of spacetime in which an object can return to its own past, tracing a trajectory that curves back on itself. In practical terms this means that time can, locally, fold in a loop and allow events to repeat or intersect with themselves.

But what if this could be applied to the real world? How would anything interact with itself from the future?

.~.

I arrived at the lab early before the hum of the city had fully seeped through the Cambridge streets. The corridors were quiet, yet subtly off. The CTC Chamber, a brushed-steel cylinder framed with superconducting rings, seemed to pulse faintly, almost as if it were breathing. I always felt a thrill standing before it with a mix of anticipation and caution. Teaching someone to respect a closed timelike loop was like asking them to walk along the edge of a cliff while juggling. But here, the cliff was the fabric of reality itself.

Tamsin Harlow burst in before I had even finished setting my notes on the workstation. A flash of curls and enthusiasm, sketching something frantically on a tablet as she spun to face me. "Elana! Look, I think the trajectories form a spiral if we chart them over multiple iterations. See?" She thrust the tablet toward me, the lines looping in tight concentric arcs, each spiral arm slightly offset, suggesting branching possibilities.

I smiled, letting my hands hover over the tablet without touching. "Indeed. Spirals make everything look more complicated than it is, don't they?" I tapped my fingers thoughtfully against the metal railing. "Sir Isaac Newton would have loved this if he'd had a laboratory like ours. Imagine him muttering about forces and action-reaction while time itself doubled back on him."

Tamsin laughed, but her eyes were serious. "Do you think the loops will behave the same with objects that have moving parts? Or more complicated ones like living creatures?" She twirled a stylus in her fingers, clearly eager to test every boundary.

"Patience," I said gently though my voice carried the subtle amusement I always reserved for her energetic bursts. "We start small. Carefully. Observation before experimentation." I gestured toward a cup resting on the pedestal at the centre of the chamber. Its porcelain surface gleamed under the soft overhead lighting. A simple object but now a participant in a strange looping ballet.

I activated the loop. The cup disappeared for a fraction of a second, a blink in which I held my breath. Then, precisely where it had been, it reappeared. No trembling, no wobble. Just perfect, silent return. Tamsin leaned forward, scribbling in her notebook. Her pencil moved so fast it was almost a blur. "It came back! Exactly the same?"

"Exactly the same," I said, though inwardly I marvelled at the mundane miracle. This was the foundation: small objects, predictable loops. They taught discipline. They taught respect. I handed Tamsin a small mechanical toy, a simple wind-up cat. "Place it gently on the pedestal," I instructed, keeping my tone calm.

She hesitated for barely a moment before following my guidance. Her fingers trembled slightly, betraying the excitement beneath her composure. "Like this?" she asked.

"Like that," I said, smiling. "Now, step back, observe. Watch without interfering. Let the loop do the work."

As she stepped aside, I could see her energy pressing against the edges of restraint. She leaned closer, muttering numbers and hypotheses under her breath, fingers tapping the table in rhythm with her thoughts. The toy disappeared, reappeared, exactly as expected. No change, no surprises. I exhaled quietly, letting the tension ease.

"See?" I said, lowering my voice to almost a whisper. "Even the simplest action has consequences but, if we proceed gently and carefully, the loop remains stable. Observation, note-taking, reflection. These are our greatest tools."

Tamsin nodded, her fidgeting easing. "It's mesmerizing," she admitted. "I can feel the time bending even with just a cup and a toy." She tilted her head, sketching spirals around the cup's trajectory, layering arcs upon arcs. "The loops help me see the paths like footprints in snow. Each loop leaves a mark, a memory, even if it disappears."

I allowed a small, approving smile. "Exactly. And your footprints must be light. Step carefully. Let the loops guide you rather than forcing them. That is the first lesson."

As she studied her spirals, I made a few notes of my own. The lines weren't perfect yet but they were enough to map the flow of cause and effect within this confined space. Teaching Tamsin wasn't just about conveying theory. It was about instilling patience, respect and humility before something larger than ourselves. The loops would teach her that if she allowed them to.

We spent the next half hour like that. Silent observation punctuated by questions and soft guidance. Tamsin sketched, tapped and whispered hypotheses. I watched, corrected gently and encouraged reflection. Each tiny movement became a study in restraint, each glance a meditation on responsibility. Even in the hum of the chamber and the flicker of its faint lights, I felt the weight of the loops pressing softly against us and I knew that this was exactly where we needed to begin.

.~.

The first few repetitions with cups and the wind-up cat had gone smoothly. Predictable. Satisfying in their simplicity. But I knew it wouldn't stay that way for long. Complexity was the true test of a loop's temperament and Tamsin, for all her careful enthusiasm, was eager to see what happened next.

"I want to try something with moving parts," she said, already pulling a small mechanical bird from her bag. Its wings flapped weakly as if impatient for flight. "It should be perfect for testing the loop, right?"

I raised an eyebrow. "Perfect perhaps if you want surprises." I let her place it gently on the pedestal. Her fingers trembled slightly, betraying excitement. I tapped the surface lightly with my index finger. A subtle signal we used in the lab to indicate caution. "Observe first. Let the loop do the work."

She stepped back but could hardly stand still. Her eyes darted between the bird and the monitors as I activated the loop. The bird disappeared and, for a heartbeat, the chamber was still. Then, in a subtle shimmer, two birds appeared. Not identical. Each moved slightly differently with wings fluttering at uneven tempos. One tilting left while another veered right.

Tamsin gasped and nearly dropped her notebook. "Oh my god, it's multiplied!" She leaned closer, sketching rapidly across the page, tracing the paths of the duplicates as they diverged and crossed.

"Exactly," I said, keeping my tone calm even as my pulse quickened. "Simple objects travel predictably. Cups, pebbles, or the stationary wind-up cat return nearly unaltered. But complex objects with moving parts interact with the loop in ways that generate branching duplicates. Each iteration carries subtle changes and ripples of choice and movement."

Her pencil moved almost too quickly to follow, charting paths that twisted and intersected. "So each duplicate is slightly different. It's like we're seeing possibilities all at once." Her voice was half awe, half barely-contained giddiness.

I nodded and stepped closer to adjust a sensor. "Notice how even the cups behave slightly differently with each iteration? Three rotations, each just a fraction off from the last. The loop is stable but it's sensitive. These differences, though minor, are the first signs of what would happen if a human, or anything living, entered the loop."

She leaned over my shoulder, eyes wide. "It's beautiful," she whispered. "Even small differences feel significant."

I allowed a small smile. "Beautiful, yes. And dangerous if ignored. Every action within a loop leaves a trace. The more complex the object, the more pronounced the effects. Patience and care are not optional. They are the only things that prevent chaos."

Her gaze flicked to a cup near the pedestal that, when left to its own path, had rotated slightly from its previous iteration. "Even this cup," she said quietly, "has a memory of its past trips."

"Exactly." I gestured toward the tablet, showing our digital map of the chamber with overlapping trajectories. The lines weren't perfectly neat with some looping back on themselves almost imperceptibly and hinting at the repeated paths of duplicates. "This is why we map their movements. Each curve tells us how duplicates move, where interactions may occur and where instability might arise. Some paths converge again while others branch off. That's the loop's response to complexity."

Tamsin was scribbling faster now and her fingers were smudged with graphite. "Can I try moving it slightly while it's looping?" she asked, eyes bright.

I paused, fingers tapping together. "Gently. One step at a time. Any abrupt motion could send the duplicates off into unpredictable territory."

She nodded, inhaling sharply then leaned forward with deliberate care. The bird's wings stirred under her gentle nudge. The duplicates responded, slight shifts along their overlapping paths. Each change was small but visible. A tilt here or a flutter there. Her eyes widened as she observed the effects, the lesson sinking in.

I watched her, quietly proud. This was the essence of mentorship in a looped world: guidance, not interference. Patience over impatience. Awareness over impulse. Yet, the thrill of discovery still danced in her gaze.

"Look," she whispered, tracing a curve across her page, "they're interacting and overlapping but not colliding. If we keep it slow and careful, the paths adjust themselves."

"Exactly," I murmured. "The loops are forgiving up to a point. They teach us subtlety not recklessness. And right now, you are learning the first, most important rule. Respect the loop and it will respect you."

She exhaled, pencil hovering over the page, a fleeting smile playing at her lips. "I think I understand," she said. "Sort of."

I laughed softly, shaking my head. "Sort of is a beginning. That is all we need today."

For the rest of the morning, we watched the duplicates, adjusted minor placements and noted their subtle variations. Each movement carried weight, every trajectory a lesson, and in that quiet chamber with the hum of the superconducting rings as a backdrop, I could see Tamsin absorbing not just the mechanics of loops but the ethical rhythm that made them safe to explore.

By the time we paused for tea, the first lessons of branching duplications had been learned. Complexity multiplies, care stabilises and subtle patterns always emerge if one only watches closely.

.~.

The moment had come for a demonstration no cup or toy

could match. I had rehearsed it countless times, tracing trajectories, calculating risk and weighing ethics. Now at the pedestal I could feel Tamsin's eyes on me as much as the chamber's hum.

"Ready?" I asked, my voice steady.

Her excitement flickered beneath a layer of tension. She had watched the smaller duplications all morning, absorbing the lessons. Now the stakes were higher. "Ready," she said, fingers drumming the tablet.

I stepped up, anticipation pressing in my chest. The superconducting rings cast pale reflections across the steel walls. I activated the loop.

Weightlessness seized my feet, as if the world had loosened its grip. The chamber blurred, walls overlapping like faint echoes. Then the duplicates appeared. Several versions of me, each slightly altered. One hesitated, another leaned forward, a third moved in perfect sync. Every iteration carried some subtle imprint. Breath, posture or angle of gaze.

"Notice the differences," I said, adjusting my footing. "Simple objects produce simple echoes. Humans are far less predictable. Every movement generates a branching path."

Tamsin stepped forward cautiously, her usual energy muted. "It's disorienting," she said. "Like the room is stretching and folding at once."

"It is," I replied. "You must move deliberately or the duplicates will interact in ways you don't expect."

I moved slowly, each gesture minimal. My duplicates mirrored me with slight offsets. One drifted too near the pedestal; a tremor in the air and a flicker of light warned of a collision before it happened. Outside, monitors would be showing minor anomalies. Clocks stuttering, conversations overlapping, footsteps repeating.

"See?" I tapped the edge of the pedestal lightly. "Small deviations amplify. The loop is sensitive to every action. Respect it."

Tamsin nodded, breathing more slowly. She stepped up, hands clenched around her tablet. "I... think I understand. Sort of," she said, nervous excitement threading her voice.

"Sort of is enough," I said. "Start with observation. Move carefully."

She placed one foot forward then the other, her eyes scanning the room. Her duplicates appeared at once. Small, slightly off versions of herself, each reacting to her tentative steps. One raised a hand too high, another leaned too far forward. She glanced at the faint arcs etched into the floor then adjusted her posture.

"Every movement matters," I murmured. "Even hesitation. You are influencing the loop."

Her pencil scratched across her notebook, tracing arcs to match the duplicates' paths. "I can see patterns," she whispered. "Not perfect, but they're there. Like I can plan my steps around the echoes."

"Exactly." I guided her, showing how to pause between motions and let the loop complete a cycle before stepping again. "Deliberation stabilises. Recklessness destabilises. Follow the markings with minimal interference and the loop will respect you."

She shifted her weight slowly, adjusting gestures and beginning to anticipate the branching echoes. Her restlessness turned to quiet concentration. Occasionally a curve of trajectory hinted at the loops' subtle geometry underfoot.

"Fascinating," she said, sketching another line. "Like walking through layers of possibility."

"Yes," I replied, smiling despite my focus. "Layers of possibility. That is the essence of a closed timelike loop. Each layer responds to your behaviour. Every action sends ripples outward."

For several minutes we moved in measured steps, observing duplicates, making small adjustments. The chamber hummed, lights flickered, but stability held. Outside, technicians murmured about minor overlaps, but nothing dangerous emerged. Tamsin's careful approach maintained equilibrium.

When we stepped down, I exhaled. She looked at me with a mix of awe and relief. "I think I understand a little more," she said.

"You do," I replied. "The loop is not to be conquered or rushed. It is to be respected, observed, allowed to teach. Now you've seen its lessons at human scale."

As we left the pedestal, the chamber's hum softened. Faint impressions of our movements lingered. The loops had spoken and for the first time Tamsin had truly listened.

.~.

After the human trial, we sat at the workbench while the chamber's hum faded to a background thrum. Tamsin's hair was mussed from leaning over the pedestal and her notebook was crowded with arcs, sketches, and half-finished equations.

"Alright," I said, lifting a cup from the bench. "The most important lesson: consequences. Even the smallest object handled carelessly can leave echoes."

She leaned forward. "Echoes?"

"Minor duplications, stray interactions. You saw the monitors, clocks stuttering and conversations overlapping. Tiny disturbances that if unchecked can spread." I set the cup down with a tap. "Watch."

Tamsin grabbed it, too quick. A moment later two cups shimmered into view. They wobbled and nudged one another with a faint clink. She gasped and nearly knocked her pencil over.

I chuckled. "Accidental duplication. Harmless here but imagine the scale with a person."

She stared, half-fascinated, half-unnerved. "So even a small mistake can cascade?"

"Exactly. Curiosity must be paired with responsibility. Every action in a loop is amplified. Intent and outcome don't always match."

Her brow furrowed. "What if we make a serious mistake?"

"Then we respond deliberately. Observe, note, correct. Panic multiplies instability. Measured action restores balance. You saw that today. Patience, observation and humility. That is the model."

She scribbled quickly. "It's like a conversation. We act, the loop replies then the result lies between the two."

"Precisely. The more complex the object, or the person, the more intricate the dialogue. Even a cup carries ripples." I tapped the table so one of the cups wobbled toward the other before settling. "Nothing is isolated."

Her smile brightened. "I understand. Sort of perfectly."

I let her enjoy the moment. "Sort of perfectly is exactly right. That's enough for today."

In the quiet, with two cups wobbling harmlessly before us, I knew the lesson had taken hold. Curiosity and caution, intent and consequence. They belonged together. Under our guidance, the loops would continue to show us how.

.~.

The next morning, as we prepared the chamber, the anomalies began to spread beyond its walls. A corridor light flickered twice in quick succession. Footsteps echoed even after the corridor was empty. A technician swore he'd answered the same question twice, in identical words.

Tamsin looked up from her notes, eyes wide. "It's happening outside now, isn't it?"

"Yes," I said. "The loops don't end at the pedestal. Every action we take pushes outward. The larger and more complex the experiment, the more threads of reality it tugs."

She turned a page, sketching quick lines across her notebook. "So even when we're not inside, the loops still ripple through the building?"

"They ripple through everything," I replied. "Which is why discipline matters. If we're careless, the disturbances will grow."

For once she was quiet, chewing the end of her pencil. Then: "Then let's learn to guide them. If we can't contain them, maybe we can teach them to behave."

Her phrasing made me smile. "Exactly. Not containment, but guidance."

The faint tremors in the building, the repeating sounds, the flicker of lights were warnings. The work ahead would no longer be about cups or toys. It would be about learning to live inside the loops without tearing the world around us.

.~.

By the afternoon the chamber felt different, as though it were listening. The hum of the superconducting rings was steady, but beneath it I sensed a readiness. We had dealt with cups, toys, even human echoes. Now came the test: could we guide several elements together without tipping the balance?

"Tamsin," I said, "this will demand everything you've learned. One action at a time. Careful and deliberate."

She nodded, more composed than when she first arrived. Excitement lingered in her eyes but now it was tempered by thought. She set her notebook aside and checked the array of objects. Two cups, the wind-up bird and the robotic device, each positioned with unusual precision.

When I activated the loop, duplicates shimmered into being. The cups rotated in place, the bird flapped, the robot wheeled forward cautiously. I braced for chaos, but the paths held steady. Branches diverged then bent back, avoiding collision.

"Notice?" I said quietly. "We're not forcing them. We've given them space, and they choose the easier path."

Tamsin's gaze flicked from the pedestal to the floor markings, faint curves etched where earlier trajectories had settled. "It's like they're falling into place on their own," she said.

"Because you're guiding with patience, not impulse. That difference is everything."

She stepped closer, adjusted the robot's wheel by a fraction and waited. The duplicates swerved then aligned. She grinned, not in triumph but in recognition. "They're listening."

"They are responding," I corrected gently. "Every ripple meets another. Guidance is a conversation, not a command."

For several minutes we worked in rhythm. I observed, suggested, corrected. She adjusted with increasing assurance. The duplicates branched, curved and then merged again. Each cycle smoother than the last. Even the faint human echoes, shadows of my own movements, folded neatly into the pattern.

Outside the chamber, lights flickered but quickly steadied. The footsteps in the corridor resolved into silence. The building itself seemed to relax.

Tamsin scribbled a quick diagram on her tablet of overlapping arcs converging toward the centre. Not a perfect spiral, but close enough to suggest order emerging from disorder. "It feels right," she said softly. "Like the loops want balance if we give them the chance."

I found myself smiling. "That's the lesson. Complexity need not mean chaos. Branching doesn't have to end in collision. Respectful guidance creates harmony."

She looked at the duplicates circling calmly. "I didn't think I could do this when I walked in. I thought I'd just... break things."

"Breaking is easy," I said. "The skill lies in holding something fragile without crushing it. That is what the loops teach."

We shut the system down slowly and let the last echoes fade before stepping off the platform. Tamsin gathered her notebook, still watching the empty pedestal as though duplicates might linger.

"You've learned what many never do," I said. "That mastery

isn't control. It's patience. The universe responds to gentle hands."

She gave a small, thoughtful nod. "Then that's how we'll treat it. Like something alive."

I didn't argue. In a way, she was right.

.~.

Outside the chamber, the traces were clear. A corridor lamp flickered twice. A notebook shifted a fraction on a desk. Footsteps echoed in the hall when it was empty. Small things but impossible to ignore.

Tamsin noticed them first. "It's spreading, isn't it?"

"Yes," I said. "The loops don't stay in the chamber. They leave impressions. Tiny and harmless for now but real."

She opened her notebook and began listing them: lights, footsteps, displaced objects. "There's a pattern. We could predict when and where they'll appear."

"Prediction is possible," I admitted. "But prediction carries responsibility. You can't chart echoes without deciding how to use them."

That slowed her hand for a moment. "You mean whether to fix them or exploit them?"

"Exactly."

We walked the lab in silence. The effects were everywhere once you looked. Monitors flickering, a pencil rolling uphill or a plant leaning toward a false light. The world was registering our work faintly but insistently.

At the window I thought of Newton. His laws explained motion with certainty yet here was motion that broke its own order and demanded an ethic. I could imagine him frowning at the data then smiling despite himself at the paradox.

Tamsin followed my gaze. "Spirals everywhere," she said, half-joking. "In the echoes, the patterns, even the way things settle back again."

I smiled. "That's how you know the lesson has taken hold.

When you see it without trying."

Her sketches told the same story. Not scattered lines anymore but arcs converging, recording not just events but her changed way of looking.

"Teaching you," I said, "has reminded me that patience is less important than clarity. The loops are not puzzles to solve but partners you live alongside."

She gave me a small nod, uncharacteristically quiet. Then almost to herself: "Every choice leaves a mark."

"Yes," I said. "And you're learning how to walk among them."

.~.

The chamber still hums quietly in its Cambridge lab. The loops remain, controlled but never erased. To most of the world they are invisible and glimpsed only in the odd flicker of a lamp or the sense of déjà vu in a corridor. Few notice and fewer understand.

Tamsin has carried the lessons forward. Her notebooks are filled with experiments I can no longer keep pace with, though every page shows the discipline she learned here: observe, guide, respect. She has grown from reckless energy into a scientist who knows that discovery is never free of consequence.

Occasionally I return to the lab. I see the faint impressions the loops leave behind. A clock skipping a beat, a headline appearing a moment early, a colleague swearing they've had the same conversation twice. These are not dangers now but reminders.

Once, in the margin of her notes, Tamsin sketched a single spiral, just one. She smiled when I noticed it. "So I don't forget," she said. The shape was less a diagram than a memory: the image of branching paths guided back toward harmony.

That is the heart of it. The loops are not rivers sweeping us along but lattices we must tread with care. Every action marks them and every choice leaves a trace.

I am content knowing that she, and others who follow, will carry this forward. The world may not yet see what we learned in that humming chamber but one day perhaps it will understand that time—flexible, fragile, endlessly echoing —is ours to navigate only with thoughtfulness, respect, and humility.

7. VULCAN'S SHADOW

For centuries, Mercury's orbit puzzled astronomers until Einstein's general relativity explained its peculiar precession and eliminated the need for a hidden planet once called Vulcan. Yet new mysteries remain such as dark matter, an unseen substance shaping galaxies, detectable only through gravity.

But what if a world made of dark matter truly circled within our own solar system, invisible to every telescope yet guiding the dance of planets and satellites through its silent pull?

.~.

I have spent most of my career staring at Mercury though never through the eyepiece of a telescope. To me it was not a gleaming planet or a symbol of speed but a puzzle. A stubborn leftover in the equations of motion. Einstein had supposedly closed the case more than a century ago, showing that general relativity explained the precession of Mercury's orbit. Yet I kept finding myself pulled back to the numbers, to the faint irregularities that even relativity did not fully smooth away.

It began innocently enough as most obsessions do. I was

reviewing a set of orbital tracking data from ESA. The kind of dry telemetry that only a handful of us enjoy. Most people look for signals of asteroids or planetary alignment shifts but I was tracing the wobble of Mercury's path. That's when I saw it. A deviation so small it might have been noise but repeating often enough to defy dismissal. Not a flaw in the detector. Not a miscalculation in timing. Something else.

The first time I noticed it I told myself to let it go. The second time I began drafting equations. By the third I was lying awake at night with planetary orbits glowing on the ceiling of my mind and convinced there was a presence unaccounted for in our neat solar system.

The notion was almost laughable. Astronomers in the 1800s had once proposed a planet, Vulcan, to explain Mercury's quirks. They imagined it tucked just inside Mercury's orbit, forever hidden in the glare of the Sun. Einstein had swept that away, his equations rendering Vulcan unnecessary. Yet here I was, more than a century later, sketching models of a planet no one had ever seen.

But this Vulcan was not the one they dreamed of. I realised it could not be hidden by geometry nor eclipsed by solar brilliance. The only explanation was stranger. Vulcan was invisible not because of where it was but because of what it was. Dark matter.

The thought chilled me and thrilled me in equal measure. A whole planet made of the very substance that shapes galaxies yet evades every attempt at direct detection. Invisible to every telescope and transparent to every wavelength. No reflection, no absorption, no shadow. A world that could pass between Earth and the Sun without the slightest interruption of light.

The more I turned the idea over in my mind, the more it explained. The precession of Mercury was only the beginning. Satellites passing through the inner system had registered tiny trajectory anomalies, adjustments dismissed as thruster misfires or computational rounding. When I applied Vulcan's mass to my models, those anomalies lined up like beads on a string. It was as though the data had been whispering its presence all along, waiting for someone stubborn enough to listen.

I remember one evening at the Royal Observatory in Greenwich, hunched over the simulations until my coffee went cold. The great dome above me felt like a vault, pressing down with the weight of centuries of astronomers who had searched the heavens and declared them complete. I could almost hear them scoffing at my persistence. Yet in the numbers, the wobble persisted like the faintest tremor of an unseen companion tugging at the planets.

I named it Vulcan although I knew the choice would raise eyebrows. The old name carried with it the embarrassment of a disproved idea. But I could not resist the poetry of reclaiming it. Not as the phantom hidden by the Sun but as something far stranger, a planet that cannot shine.

I had learned enough to know I could not pursue this alone. My models needed scrutiny by someone rigorous enough to test every parameter. I thought immediately of Professor Asha Rey. Her work on dark matter distributions was meticulous, her caution bordering on severity. She had little patience for loose speculation which was precisely why I needed her.

I drafted the message carefully and attached my calculations with a mixture of pride and trepidation. Then I stared out of the observatory window where London's lights muddied the stars. Somewhere out there, between us and the Sun, an unseen world was orbiting. No telescope would ever capture it yet its hand was written into the orbits of Mercury and Venus like a watermark.

As I pressed send, I felt the strange duality of discovery. The solitude of knowing something no one else quite believes and the anticipation of seeing whether the universe had at last revealed a new companion.

.~.

Professor Asha Rey had seen her share of eccentric proposals.

Over the years, she had been sent theories about hollow planets, mirrored universes and particles that bent causality itself. Most of them barely survived a first reading. Yet Rowan Pritchard's message lingered in her mind long after she had opened it.

It was not the claim that caught her attention, an invisible planet, made entirely of dark matter, orbiting between Mercury and the Sun. Such an idea was almost designed to trigger scepticism. What held her was the precision of his calculations. The numbers were careful, consistent and, unlike so many unsolicited theories, seemed to be grounded in real data.

She cleared her desk at Cambridge that evening, set aside the graduate essays waiting for her review and loaded Rowan's orbital models into her own software. Hours later, the office was silent except for the hum of the machines and the faint scratching of her pen as she checked figures by hand.

Rowan's anomalies aligned too neatly to ignore. Mercury's residual precession, the unexplained trajectory nudges in satellite records and even slight perturbations in Venus's orbit, traced a pattern that was unlikely to be coincidence.

Still, she distrusted neatness. It was her instinct, honed through years of research, to look for the flaw in the picture. She re-ran his models under different assumptions of planetary mass and solar oblateness, even under contrived error scenarios. Each time, Vulcan's gravitational fingerprint emerged again.

By midnight she was forced to concede there was something there. Not proof, not yet, but enough to warrant further investigation.

Log entry, Sol 241:

Cross-checked Pritchard's orbital simulations. Residuals consistent across three independent datasets. Hypothesis: inner solar system body composed of non-luminous matter. Unusual but mathematically coherent. Probability of artefact <0.02.

Note: remain cautious.

When she finally called Rowan, she was brisk. "Your models are elegant," she admitted, "but elegance doesn't make them correct. If Vulcan exists, it would have to be dynamically stable. And stability in the inner solar system is not trivial."

Rowan smiled faintly at her severity even through the screen. "That's why I sent it to you. You're the one who will find the error if there is one."

She appreciated the trust though she did not say so. Over the following weeks their collaboration deepened, a rhythm of equations and simulations passed back and forth across secure channels. Rowan provided intuition, noticing when a tiny deviation hinted at something larger. Asha provided rigour, subjecting every parameter to relentless testing.

It was during one of these long exchanges that she caught herself describing Vulcan not as an anomaly but as a presence. The shift unsettled her. Scientists, she reminded herself, should not anthropomorphise equations. Yet the more they refined the orbit, the clearer Vulcan's influence became as though it were quietly sculpting the solar system from the shadows.

Rowan seemed almost enchanted. "It's like an invisible hand," he said one evening, his tone reverent.

Asha shook her head. "Invisible hands are metaphors. What we have is a mass distribution consistent with dark matter. Nothing more."

But when she ended the call, she lingered over the orbital plots still glowing on her monitor. Each line curved in precise synchrony, and the pattern was oddly beautiful.

Together they tested the limits of Vulcan's stability. If its mass were too great, it would disrupt Earth's orbit. Too small, and its effect on Mercury would vanish. The sweet spot they uncovered was uncanny: a narrow range of mass and distance in which Vulcan's gravity explained every residual without causing chaos.

It was still not proof. But it was enough to make her wonder.

Asha closed her logbook that night with deliberate care, pressing the pen mark flat against the page. In her official notes she kept her language dry but privately she felt a flicker of something else. Curiosity, edged with unease. A planet that could never be seen, orbiting silently yet guiding the dance of worlds.

She set her alarm for an early meeting and turned off the lights. As the office darkened, the plots of Vulcan's orbit lingered on her mind. A silent curve threading through the heart of the solar system. A reminder that the universe often keeps its deepest truths just beyond the reach of light.

.~.

The conference hall in London was brighter than Asha preferred. Spotlights glared across polished glass and steel, designed to impress visiting dignitaries but unkind to speakers who valued clarity over theatre. She glanced at Rowan as they waited to present and saw him fidgeting with his notes, eyes distant. He looked less like a man about to argue for a hidden planet and more like someone listening for faint music only he could hear.

Asha reminded herself that she was here to ground his intuition in the firmest data possible. She had vetted the models, re-run the simulations and stripped away every unnecessary flourish. What remained was not proof. but it was persuasive.

When the chair called them forward, Rowan spoke first. His voice carried a quiet certainty. "Ladies and gentlemen," he began, "we may have discovered a planet entirely invisible to light, orbiting within the inner solar system." He gestured to a projected diagram. Mercury's elliptical path traced in pale white. "Its effects are subtle, measurable only through gravitational residuals. Yet once included, the anomalies vanish. The orbit closes."

Murmurs rose from the audience. Asha took over with her tone clipped and professional. "We are not speaking of a hidden sphere in the glare of the Sun as nineteenth-century astronomers once imagined. This body, if it exists, is made of non-luminous matter, transparent to every wavelength. Its gravitational effects, however, are consistent across multiple datasets."

She paused, letting the numbers on the screen settle. Perihelion shifts, residual plots, error bars narrow and neat. It was the data that mattered, not the drama.

The first question came from a grey-haired man in the second row. "Could these residuals not be computational artefacts?"

Asha answered calmly. "We considered that. Three independent orbital models, processed with different assumptions, yield the same anomaly. The signal persists."

Rowan leaned forward. "The elegance of general relativity remains intact. Vulcan does not break the theory. It extends our application of it."

The word "Vulcan" caused a ripple. Some nodded at the historical resonance while others looked sceptical, perhaps thinking of past embarrassments. Asha kept her expression neutral. Naming mattered less than consistency.

Another voice called out. "If it is dark matter, why should it form a planet at all? Isn't dark matter diffuse?"

"That is a valid challenge," Asha conceded. "Our models suggest a compact distribution, possibly bound through early solar dynamics. It is unconventional but not impossible."

For half an hour they fielded questions, Rowan steady in his quiet conviction, Asha exact in her replies. By the end, the room had not been won over but it had been unsettled. And that, she knew, was sometimes the best result. Science advanced by discomfort.

That evening, in the quiet of her hotel room, Asha wrote another log entry.

Log entry, Sol 248:

Conference response mixed. Some scepticism, some interest. Observers unsettled by the notion of an invisible inner planet. Pritchard more persuasive than anticipated — his tone carries conviction. I remain cautious. Data consistent but extraordinary claims demand extraordinary proof.

She closed the notebook and looked out at the Thames where the city lights shimmered across the water. It struck her that the river too concealed hidden currents beneath its glittering surface. The visible and the invisible shaping one another.

Rowan's words echoed in her mind: *an invisible hand moving through spacetime.* She would never phrase it so loosely yet she could not deny the image stayed with her.

Tomorrow they would return to simulations and to refining the orbit. For now, she allowed herself a rare admission. The possibility of Vulcan was beautiful in its quiet defiance of visibility.

.~.

I had not expected the story to travel so fast. Conferences are usually slow burners: papers trickle into proceedings, summaries appear in niche journals and only occasionally does an idea escape into wider view. Vulcan, however, seemed to catch fire overnight.

The first headline I saw, scrolling on my phone over breakfast, was dramatic: **"Earth's Dark Twin Haunts the Inner Solar System."** It was accompanied by an artist's impression of a glowing black sphere, haloed in warped starlight. Nothing in our data looked remotely like that, of course, but accuracy was never the media's first instinct.

By the following week, the tide of speculation was unstoppable. Newspapers spoke of a "ghost planet" that could lurk between us and the Sun. Some broadcasters interviewed astrologers, of all people, eager to know what influence

Vulcan might exert over human destiny. Children's magazines printed colourful spreads of an invisible world teeming with imagined dark-matter lifeforms.

I tried, at first, to correct the record. "It is not hidden," I explained patiently to one reporter. "It is fundamentally transparent. You cannot draw what cannot be seen." But metaphors have more power than footnotes and the public preferred shadows and spectres to careful distinctions.

Asha handled it better. In interviews she was precise and measured, never drifting beyond what the equations justified. "There is no danger," she told a BBC panel, her tone firm but calm. "Vulcan's orbit is stable. Its influence is subtle. The solar system remains exactly as it has always been. We have simply learned to describe it more completely."

I admired her restraint although I sensed the effort it cost. When the cameras switched off she would sigh faintly as though the weight of public imagination pressed heavier than any calculation.

For me, the fascination of others was almost beside the point. What mattered was the pattern itself. The way Mercury's orbit, when plotted with Vulcan included, finally closed into harmony. There was something deeply satisfying about that symmetry like hearing a discord resolve into music.

Still, I could not avoid the cultural swell. Walking along the Thames one evening, I passed a street artist selling sketches to tourists. Among his usual Big Ben and Tower Bridge scenes was a drawing of a dark, featureless planet, half-shaded in charcoal. "The invisible world," he told me proudly, as if he had glimpsed it himself. I almost bought the picture but stopped. It felt too strange to hold an imagined image of something I had argued could never be seen.

Asha and I continued our simulations amid the noise. The models grew more refined and the orbit more certain. Each adjustment brought Vulcan into sharper mathematical relief. Yet the world outside our equations was spinning its own stories. Some spoke of hidden dangers while others spoke of secret guardianship. One columnist declared that Vulcan was proof the universe was designed with mysteries to keep humanity humble.

I should have been irritated. Yet, in an odd way the public response mirrored my own private awe. They were wrong in detail but not in spirit. Vulcan was a reminder that reality extends beyond sight, that absence of evidence is not evidence of absence.

Late at night, when the calculations blurred, I would imagine standing on a cliff at dawn, the Sun rising bright and indifferent and somewhere in that glare an unseen planet tracing its path. It would never shine, never cast a shadow, never announce itself. Yet its gravity would be there, tugging gently, shaping the solar system's dance.

Perhaps that was why the story took hold. We are drawn to the unseen, to the possibility that beneath appearances something else is guiding the pattern. For centuries, people had looked up at Mercury's stubborn orbit and wondered. Now we were offering an answer. Not a planet of fire or rock but a world that was nothing but gravity and silence.

The irony was not lost on me. I had started this search in the solitude of raw numbers, chasing anomalies most would dismiss. Now, Vulcan had escaped into the imagination of millions. It was no longer mine nor even ours. It belonged to the human hunger for mystery.

Perhaps that was fitting. After all, I reminded myself as I turned back towards the observatory, Vulcan was never meant to be seen. It was meant to be felt: In the tug of Mercury's precession, in the whisper of satellite clocks and in the quiet wonder of knowing that reality is always deeper than the light will show.

.~.

It was Rowan who first noticed the anomaly. He arrived at Cambridge with a stack of satellite reports, eyes bright from a sleepless night.

"Look at these clocks," he said, tapping the figures. "They're off. Not by much, only nanoseconds. But always in the same region, near Vulcan's projected orbit."

Asha skimmed the tables. A billionth of a second here, another there. Easy to dismiss. "Atomic clocks are sensitive. Thermal drift, relativistic corrections"

Rowan shook his head. "Except scatter doesn't line up like this. Different satellites, different missions. Yet the same lag."

She re-ran the numbers herself. The offsets persisted. If real, Vulcan was not only tugging at orbits but bending time locally.

Her instinct was to resist. The hypothesis was already extraordinary; layering time dilation onto it would sound fantastical. But the pattern was stubborn, repeating across independent datasets.

At their next seminar Rowan put it simply. "The clocks tick slower here," he told the audience. Murmurs spread. Asha intervened crisply. "We suggest no exotic mechanism. Clumped dark matter could distort spacetime unevenly. But the sample size is small. More data is required."

She knew her role: to tether the discussion. Rowan knew his too: to see the pattern.

Later, crossing the quad, he said, "You're right to be cautious. But you felt it, didn't you? That flicker of possibility."

She exhaled. "Possibility is not proof."

He smiled. "That's why we work well together."

They worked the anomaly into their paper only cautiously, a footnote among orbital parameters and error bars. Asha wrote the abstract herself, clipped and formal. No metaphors, no speculation. Just residuals, models, and margins.

To their surprise, the reviewers accepted it as plausible. Vulcan was mathematically coherent, though invisible. Space agencies began applying subtle corrections to trajectories. Astrophysicists asked whether other systems might hide similar planets.

Educators turned Vulcan into a lesson: that unseen forces can shape the world. Children sketched dark globes haloed with stars. Rowan smiled at their mistakes, noting they were wrong in detail but right in spirit.

Log entry, Sol 312:

Publication accepted. Subsequent studies underway. Vulcan remains unobservable. Data consistent. Hypothesis stands, for now.

For Asha, that was enough. A balance between belief and doubt. For Rowan, it was something quieter. The satisfaction of having traced an invisible spiral in the solar system's dance and shown that mystery still breathes within the ordinary.

.~.

I walk the Thames most evenings now. The river is a quiet companion, its currents steady, unseen flows shaping what lies above. It reminds me of the data that first caught my eye. Faint anomalies in Mercury's orbit, easy to overlook yet insistent once noticed. Those traces have grown into something far larger than I imagined.

Asha calls it an achievement though she never overstates it. To her Vulcan is a hypothesis. Supported for now but awaiting challenge. She is right of course. Science demands caution. Yet walking here, under lamplight on the water, I allow myself a moment of wonder.

Vulcan will never be seen. If it passed between Earth and the Sun tomorrow, the sky would remain unchanged. No telescope will capture it. Its reality lies only in the paths it bends. Like Mercury's precession, Venus's orbit or the drift of satellite clocks, it exists in inference, not in vision.

There is poetry in that. We think of knowledge as light yet Vulcan shows that truth can also be shadow, grasped only through the motions it sets in play.

I sometimes picture children sketching the "dark planet" as

a black globe haloed with stars. Wrong in detail, perhaps, but not in spirit. For them, as for me, it is a reminder that discovery does not end with what our eyes can see.

Sometimes late at night, I sketch Mercury's orbit. The ellipse that refuses to close until Vulcan's gravity brings it into harmony. That spiral trace, curving just enough to reveal a hidden companion, is still to me the most elegant signature in astronomy.

As I lean against the railing, the river rippling dark below, I know Vulcan is circling even now, silent and invisible. It will never shine, never cast a shadow, yet it shapes the world all the same.

That, I think, is its gift. A reminder that reality is larger than light. Vulcan does not need to be seen to be real. It only needs to be felt in the way the universe moves.

8. HUBBLE'S TENSION

Astronomers face a puzzle at the edge of understanding. When they measure the expansion rate of the universe nearby, by observing galaxies and supernovae, they find a value that is about ten percent higher than when they infer it from the early universe's afterglow. This disagreement, known as the Hubble tension, has resisted explanation despite years of careful work.

One possibility is that the energy of empty space, so-called dark energy, is not fixed at all. What if it seeps into the cosmos little by little, too slowly to notice except across cosmic time? And what if this drip of dark energy were not smooth but came in tiny packets. Quanta so small and rare that only the most delicate experiment could ever hope to catch them?

.~.

T he lab was quiet except for the low hum of the cryocooler idling in the corner and the faint tick of the wall clock. Most of the building had emptied hours ago. Through the tall windows, London's sky was the colour of slate, the city lights haloed by a fine mist.

Elara Quinn sat at the long bench with her hands clasped

around a cooling mug of tea. Papers were spread before her, graphs half-obscured by pencilled notes. Across from her, Tamsin Harlow had a laptop open, the glow reflected in her glasses. She tapped at the trackpad then sat back and exhaled through her nose.

"Still the same," she said. "Planck versus late-universe. The numbers refuse to agree."

Elara didn't answer right away. She reached for a pencil, turned a sheet of paper sideways and sketched two lines. One neat and steady, the other peeling away ever so slightly. "Early measurements say seventy. Local ones say closer to seventy-seven. Ten percent. Not noise, not calibration. Something real."

Tamsin leaned forward, chin on her hand. "We've been through every systematic. Dust, Cepheid metallicities, selection bias. Nothing's big enough to close the gap."

Elara looked past the paper toward the dark window. "Then maybe it isn't an error. Maybe something changes between then and now."

Tamsin gave a wry smile. "You're suggesting dark energy isn't constant. Lambda's grave is already crowded with theories."

"Not a grave," Elara said softly. "A placeholder. A symbol for what we don't understand."

Tamsin folded her arms. "If dark energy varies then it does so below any instrument's reach. The density today is six times ten to the minus ten joules per cubic metre. To nudge expansion by ten percent over the age of the universe, the change per second would be unimaginably small."

Elara picked up her mug, sipped, grimaced at the taste. "But not zero. Over billions of years then even a whisper accumulates."

Tamsin studied her, then the sketch. "A whisper you think we can hear?"

"Maybe not hear," Elara said, "but sense. If it isn't a smooth flow but something discrete. Say tiny packets shed from the vacuum itself." She tapped the paper with her pencil. "Energy arriving in quanta. Too small to see at once but building steadily."

Tamsin frowned but her tone softened. "Packets of dark energy. You'd need a name for them."

Elara allowed herself the faintest smile. "One will come."

They fell into silence again. The laptop's cooling fan whirred and the clock ticked. Outside mist swirled around the lamps along the street.

At last Tamsin closed the computer. "If there is such a drip, it's below the threshold of detection. But maybe..." she hesitated, conceding more than she had planned "maybe it's worth thinking how we might look."

Elara's pencil traced the two diverging lines once more. "The tension won't go away. It's telling us something. We just need to learn how to listen."

.~.

The next morning the lab smelled faintly of coffee and solder flux. Rain tapped the windows in an uneven rhythm and somewhere in the ducting a fan clattered against its bearings.

Tamsin stood at the whiteboard with her marker uncapped while Elara sat at the bench flipping through the notes they'd left scattered overnight. Neither had slept much but there was a light in their eyes that tiredness couldn't dim.

"Packets," Tamsin said, writing the word at the top of the board. "If the vacuum is releasing energy in discrete units, we need a scale. What size, how often, how to catch them."

Elara stirred her tea, thoughtful. "We can't know yet. But start with the Hubble tension. Ten percent of six times ten to the minus ten joules per cubic metre, spread over the universe's age. That works out to..." She reached for a calculator, tapped in figures. "About ten to the minus twenty-eight joules per cubic metre per second."

"Which is nothing," Tamsin replied, capping the marker with

a click. "Smaller than the energy of a single microwave photon by orders of magnitude."

Elara looked up. "Unless the vacuum parcels it. Not a continuous seep, but occasional packets. Each one tiny but finite. If we could count them, we'd see the drift."

Tamsin leaned against the board, arms crossed. "Alright. Let's say these packets exist. What do we call them?"

"Deons," Elara said simply.

Tamsin raised an eyebrow.

"Dark energy quanta," Elara explained. "Like photons. Like muons. Deons."

Tamsin nodded once. "Fine. Then the question is: how big is a deon?"

Elara tapped her pencil against the page. "Suppose one arrives every few seconds in a cubic metre. That would make each worth about four times ten to the minus twenty-eight joules."

"Or it could be one every second," Tamsin countered. "Or one every hour. We don't know."

"That's what the experiment must tell us."

Tamsin began sketching a sphere on the board. "One cubic metre cavity. Easy to normalise. Vacuum inside. Coat it with something superconducting, force a single high-Q resonance. Then monitor for phase drift."

Elara smiled faintly. "Always the engineer."

"Always the pragmatist," Tamsin corrected. She added rough numbers beside the drawing. "If the drip is real then it's coherent. It will integrate over time. Noise grows like the square root of time. Signal stacks linearly. Given long enough, the ratio rises and the deons show themselves."

Elara pushed her notes aside and joined her at the board. "So we build a detector. Cheap materials, whatever we can salvage. A pulse-tube cooler, some Kevlar suspension, RF reflectometry."

Tamsin nodded slowly. "We won't know the cadence until we

measure it. It could be maddeningly slow."

"Or too fast for us to isolate," Elara said.

"Either way, the distribution will tell us something." Tamsin capped the marker with a snap. "If there's nothing but noise then we'll know. If deons exist, they'll reveal themselves."

Elara glanced at the board, then hesitated. "We'll need a sphere, coatings, cryo time. I should at least mention it to Grant."

Tamsin smirked. "Your department head still remembers the tachyon proposal."

Elara sighed. "He remembers all my proposals. That's his job."

Later that afternoon she knocked on a door already ajar. Professor Grant looked up from a monitor, glasses sliding down his nose.

"Quinn," he said. "Not another crusade I hope."

"Something modest," Elara replied evenly. "An old aluminium sphere and a pulse-tube cooler. We've got most of it in storage. No new spend."

Grant eyed her for a long moment. "This isn't tachyons again is it? Or that business with negative mass?"

"Nothing so exotic," Elara said. "Just a calibration run. Noise characterisation in a cryo cavity. If we see nothing then that's the result."

He sighed, leaning back in his chair. "You have a talent for chasing ghosts Quinn. But if it costs nothing and you don't neglect your teaching load, take what you need. No requisitions, no invoices."

"Understood."

Grant waved her away already turning back to his monitor. "One day you'll learn the difference between wild theory and useful physics."

Back in the lab, Tamsin was unpacking coils of cable. "Permission granted?"

"Permission ignored," Elara said, placing the slip on the

bench. "We're to spend nothing, leave no trace and prove nothing. Should be easy."

They both laughed quietly. The rain drummed harder on the glass as though echoing their decision.

.~.

By the end of the week the lab looked less like an office and more like a garage workshop. Anodised aluminium plates leaned against the wall, a coil of Kevlar thread dangled from a hook and half-emptied coffee cups were scattered among boxes of connectors and vacuum seals.

Tamsin crouched beside the open crate of surplus hardware, tugging out a dented sphere segment. "This is the one," she said. "Leftover from a particle calibration chamber. A bit scratched but we don't need pretty."

Elara wiped her hands on a rag, eyeing the curved plate. "Can we make it airtight?"

"With enough epoxy and swearing," Tamsin replied. "We only need high vacuum, not CERN-grade."

They spent hours bolting and welding the sections together until a rough aluminium sphere, about a metre and a quarter across, sat on a foam pad in the centre of the room. It looked improvised and almost comical but the volume inside was what mattered.

The next step was coating. Elara opened a jar of the superconducting spray. An experimental compound that one of their colleagues had abandoned for being too temperamental. It clung to the metal with a dull sheen.

"It doesn't have to be perfect," she murmured, spraying slow arcs across the inner surface. "Just continuous."

"Like wallpapering a cave," Tamsin said with her head poked through the access hatch.

By evening the sphere glowed faintly under the work lights showing a patchy metallic mirror. They lowered it onto a ring stand and laced Kevlar threads through eyelets to suspend it from the ceiling.

When the cryocooler finally arrived from storage, an old two-stage pulse-tube with half the paint flaking off, Tamsin knelt to align the feed lines. "It'll never hit millikelvin but four kelvin's plenty. If the signal's real, we'll see it."

Elara watched the thermometer graph settle. "And if it isn't?"

"Then we add this to the list of ghosts."

.~.

Three nights later, Professor Grant appeared unannounced. The door creaked open and his silhouette filled the frame, the smell of pipe smoke preceding him. He looked at the suspended sphere, at the makeshift cryostat patched with aluminium tape, at the laptop balanced on a stool.

"I told you 'no requisitions'," he said.

Tamsin straightened, wiping her hands on her jeans. "Everything here is scrap, Professor. No forms filed and no money spent."

Grant stepped closer, peering at the frost halo blooming around the cooler's exhaust. "You really built it."

Elara met his gaze steadily. "We want to test a hypothesis. If nothing appears, nothing's lost."

He ran a finger across a cable tie as though checking workmanship. "Tachyons. Negative mass. Now deons. You two collect eccentricities like medals."

Tamsin grinned. "Better than collecting dust."

For a moment Grant almost smiled but he shook his head instead. "If the Dean hears of this, I will deny knowledge."

"That's all we need," Elara said.

He stood there longer, watching the slow drip of condensed vapour off the cooler. Then, with a grunt, he left without another word.

By midnight the detector was fully assembled. One coaxial line through the wall, a coupling loop and a string of amplifiers leading to their laptop. On the screen a thin trace jittered across the baseline.

Tamsin sat back, rubbing her eyes. "First light, as the astronomers say."

Elara rested her chin on her hand. "Except here we hope for first dark."

They laughed softly, the exhaustion easing just a little. The machine was alive, humming faintly, waiting.

.~.

The lab felt like a watchmaker's workshop at midnight. Hushed, meticulous, every click and hum magnified by expectation. The aluminium sphere hung motionless on its threads with, frost clinging pale to the seams. A coax led out to the bench where the laptop's trace wavered in a flat sea of noise.

Elara sat forward with elbows on her knees and eyes locked on the screen. Tamsin leaned back in her chair, pencil poised, tapping restlessly.

"Baseline's quiet," she murmured. "If there's anything here we should see it."

Half an hour passed before a flicker nudged the trace. A tiny step, barely above noise. Elara's hand darted to the notebook. "Mark it."

Another came ten minutes later. Then silence.

Tamsin frowned. "Too sparse. If deons are real, they shouldn't be this shy." She pushed back from the desk, rummaged in a drawer and produced a small shielded box bristling with connectors.

"Elaton comb filter," she explained. "Scavenged from an old resonator board. Carves the band into narrow channels. Right now we're staring wide-eyed into static. This will sharpen the view."

Elara raised an eyebrow. "You were sitting on that?"

"Always keep a joker," Tamsin said. She spliced it into the line, adjusted a bias screw and watched the analyser bloom with a comb of razor peaks. "Sixteen passbands. Each acts like an

93

independent ear."

The effect was immediate. Within minutes, the screen ticked twice in succession. Then again a few seconds later. No longer single ghosts in the noise, but a scatter of events across the channels.

Elara scribbled times into the notebook: 2.8 s, 3.4 s, 3.0 s, 3.2 s. Irregular, capricious, but falling into rhythm.

"Poisson," Tamsin said quietly. "Random arrivals. But look at the mean."

They plotted as the hours passed, the pencil columns filling. By dawn, the average had steadied. Three point one seconds.

Elara traced the numbers with her finger. "Yesterday we had nothing. Tonight we have 3.1. It's converging."

"Not fast enough," Tamsin muttered. "But tomorrow we'll open more channels. Sixty-four, maybe a hundred. Push the counts up."

The lab door creaked. Professor Grant stood just inside, coat collar turned up against the night. He glanced at the frost-bloomed sphere, the humming cooler, the crowded columns of numbers.

"You've caught something," he said, his voice unreadable.

Tamsin didn't look up. "Deons. Thousands of them. Average spacing's three point one seconds in a cubic metre."

Grant gave a short nod. "Then make it tighter. One digit won't hold a lecture. Show me two." He turned and left without another word.

Silence closed in again. Elara looked down at the notebook at the uneven tally marks that nonetheless circled a single truth.

"Three point one," she whispered.

Tamsin capped her pencil with a click. "Tomorrow it'll be three point one four." Elara raised her eyebrows.

The screen flickered. Another deon ticked into the record, right on cue.

.~.

The following week blurred into a rhythm of long nights and black coffee. Tamsin kept adding channels through the etalon comb. The old lab filled with racks of blinking SDRs and the steady wheeze of cryocoolers.

Day one, the mean sat at 3.1 seconds.

Day two, with sixteen passbands live, it tightened to 3.14.

Day three, sixty-four channels: 3.142.

Day four, with a second sphere Grant had "liberated" from storage, it nudged to 3.1417.

By the fifth day, with three spheres and a hundred passbands running in parallel, the tally circled around 3.14159.

Elara stared at the notebook, the digits lined in pencil. "This looks an awful lot like it's trending toward π."

Tamsin's smile was thin, sceptical but unable to hide a spark. "We'll let the counts tell us. More channels, more runs. No claims yet."

Grant leaned in from behind them, reading without comment. At last he said, "You've got enough for the presentation. Don't wait."

.~.

The Royal Society's hall was full. Elara began. "The expansion of the universe, measured in two epochs, disagrees by seven to ten percent. This is the Hubble tension."

Tamsin advanced the slides: battered spheres haloed in frost, superconducting coatings, Kevlar suspension, etalon combs. "We monitored the resonance phase under vacuum at cryogenic temperature and recorded discrete, repeatable increments of ~4×10^{-28} joules, which we term *deons*. Arrivals are stochastic, a Poisson process with exponentially distributed arrival times."

Then came the results. The slide showed the daily progression: $3.1 \rightarrow 3.14 \rightarrow 3.142 \rightarrow 3.1417 \rightarrow 3.14159$. The hall stirred audibly.

Elara spoke, steady but careful. "This looks an awfully lot

like it is trending towards π, but we are not claiming a universal constant. Seconds and metres are our choice, not the universe's. All we are reporting is an empirical cadence in our one-cubic-metre cavity, under stated conditions. The mean waiting time between deons converges to 3.14159 ± 0.00006 s at the 85% level, corroborated by an independent one-week high-throughput run."

The murmurs deepened.

Questions followed about thermal drift, microphonics and cosmic rays. Tamsin answered each with calibration plots and veto data. Elara repeated, "We present only the statistics. The interpretation is yours."

From the front row, Grant gave the smallest nod, as though to anchor them with his reputation.

.~.

The hall emptied slowly, clusters of physicists lingering in the aisles, voices low but animated. The slides had been switched off, the frost-coated spheres left behind in photographs, yet the numbers seemed to echo even as the lights dimmed: 3.14159.

Outside, the evening was cool and faintly damp. London traffic muttered along the Strand, headlights glinting off wet pavement. Elara and Tamsin leaned against the stone balustrade, side by side, the buzz of the session still ringing in their ears.

Tamsin folded her arms. "Well. They didn't throw fruit."

Elara smiled faintly. "They didn't cheer either."

"They're scientists. They'll chew on it for years before anyone smiles."

Silence stretched a moment. A taxi splashed past with its tyres hissing.

Elara's gaze lingered on the dark and restless river. "It shouldn't matter that the mean points to π. The units are ours to choose. There's no reason those human measures should carry the universe's imprint. But there it is, written out to five digits as if the vacuum wanted to leave a signature."

Tamsin glanced at her. "Message from the cosmos?"

Elara shook her head, but her voice softened. "Maybe just coincidence. Maybe not. What matters is that the universe doesn't just expand. It whispers while it does."

Tamsin chuckled quietly. "Don't let Grant hear you call it whispering."

As if on cue, the man himself emerged from the doors, coat draped over one arm. He paused beside them with eyes as unreadable as ever.

"You'll be attacked for this," he said. "Your calculations will be pulled apart and every decimal tested. Good. That's the only way discoveries live."

Tamsin tilted her head. "And you?"

Grant looked out across the city lights. For once there was no trace of weariness and only the faintest curve at the corner of his mouth. "Me? I'll enjoy being in the acknowledgements. Don't ruin it with tachyons."

He walked away, leaving them with the river and the night.

Elara exhaled slowly. "We've measured something that shouldn't exist in isolation and yet it does. The tiniest drip, feeding the universe."

Tamsin nodded, thoughtful. "Deons. Quietest things we've ever caught and loud enough to shift cosmology."

They stood in silence, watching the lights ripple across the water. For the first time in weeks there was no hurry, only the quiet astonishment of having measured what should have been beyond reach. A number had risen out of the dark. Not arbitrary, not ragged but familiar and almost intimate.

Elara's voice was barely above a whisper. "Maybe it's nothing more than chance. But if the universe does keep time, then π is a rhythm it seems to know by heart."

Tamsin said nothing yet she smiled and in that silence the city seemed to breathe in time with them. Steady, measured and infinite.

9. ENTROPY'S CHILDREN

The "arrow of time" is marked by entropy, the steady drift from order to disorder. Cups shatter but never reassemble, smoke disperses but never regathers, ice melts but does not refreeze on its own. Yet the fundamental laws of physics are time-symmetric. They do not forbid processes running backwards. On paper, entropy could fall instead of rise.

What would life look like if that symmetry were real? If disaster was not a conclusion but the first step and memory flowed away from what we call the past?

.~.

T he survey ship Hesper was built for dependable work. Its missions were meant to be steady and unremarkable: orbital mapping, mineral surveys, supply drops. The crew of six expected Enceladus to be another routine entry on the list. Then the signal arrived.

It was faint but regular, a pulse repeating through the static. The pattern matched a distress beacon last used half a century earlier. Station Janus. The research base had been declared lost when seismic shifts sealed it beneath the ice. Records closed the file with regret. Nothing could have survived. Yet the beacon pulsed on.

Commander Asha Rey studied the readings in silence. Power signatures. Structural echoes. Heat traces. All impossible yet consistent. Against expectation the outpost endured. She considered for only a moment before giving the order.

"Prepare descent capsule. Leon, Imogen. With me."

The capsule detached with a jolt. Its nose dipped toward the fissures below. Enceladus filled the viewport with a pale world scarred by cracks and scored by fountains of vapour. Plumes of ice arched into space glittering faintly in Saturn's distant light.

The entry tunnel was narrow. Its walls were carved by geysers and braced long ago by human hands. Steel struts still held the ice in place, their surfaces too clean to be fifty years old. Floodlights picked out veins of salt and trapped bubbles as they descended deeper into the crust.

Leon Ortega bent over the controls. He called out each figure twice, a habit the others had learned to trust. "Trajectory steady. Lock confirmed. Still steady." When the capsule jolted he added dryly, "Enceladus likes to remind us who's in charge."

Imogen Vance leaned close to the viewport. Her breath misted the glass as she watched the frozen walls slip past. She carried a small notebook on her lap, already open to a blank page. She sketched quickly with her pencil darting across the paper. Though more than once she lifted her head too soon, unwilling to miss the view.

The clamps struck with a metallic thud. Status lights flicked green in sequence: atmosphere stable, oxygen rich, gravity calibrated. Each reading defied reason.

The airlock opened. Warm air drifted in, tinged with ozone and a metallic tang, like iron on the tongue. Asha moved first, her pace steady, her stillness a signal to the others. The corridor beyond glowed with light. Surfaces were polished, conduits hummed softly and the air felt as if the station had only just been built. A figure waited.

A woman stood in the passageway, composed and still. She neither flinched nor smiled, as though the moment was already familiar. Her gaze swept across the three visitors, calm and assured.

"I am Director Kael," she said. Her voice was even, her presence steady. "We are relieved you are departing."

The words rang strangely in the quiet. Asha frowned. "Departing? We have only just arrived."

Kael inclined her head, sorrow shadowing her eyes. "From our side, you have already left."

Silence filled the corridor. Leon checked his wrist display, as if numbers might bend time into sense. Imogen's pencil hung above the page, a line half-drawn. Asha stood motionless but her thoughts were sharp behind her calm.

Station Janus had begun to tell its story and the story ran in reverse.

.~.

At first sight, Station Janus looked ordinary. Corridors were bright, the air was temperate, machinery hummed with steady rhythm. Yet the absence of age was more unsettling than decay would have been. Nothing carried the mark of fifty years sealed in ice.

Director Kael led them on without comment. Asha Rey's eyes were moving constantly as she followed a pace behind. She noted polished walls, flooring without scuffs, conduits clean as new. Not signs of survival but of renewal.

Leon Ortega carried his handheld with his eyes fixed on its screen. He checked the figures aloud then repeated them as if saying them twice forced them to hold. "Power steady. Pressure balanced. Still steady." The habit steadied him more than the readings themselves.

Imogen Vance walked with her notebook open still sketching the lines of the corridor. But often, when she looked back, her marks seemed oddly placed as though her hand had drawn them before she intended. She blamed fatigue but felt a gnawing unease.

The central dome stopped them in their tracks. Artificial sunlight bathed gardens of herbs and grain. People moved at a calm pace, unhurried and serene.

Children played in the courtyard. A boy tossed a ball yet it landed in his friend's hands before it left his own. Laughter followed, natural in sound but unnatural in sequence.

In the gardens, workers tended plants with quiet focus. Where their fingers touched, stems rose rather than fell, cuttings fusing back onto stalks. Leaves uncurled into wholeness.

In the workshops, technicians guided fragments back together. A shattered panel rose from the floor, pieces sliding into place until the crack was gone. The workers did not marvel. To them it was routine.

Imogen stopped, staring. "Did you see that?"

Leon gave a tight smile. "If my kitchen worked like this, I would never wash a mug again." His tone tried for humour but strain edged his words.

The mess hall deepened their unease. Plates and trays lay scattered with scraps: crusts, bones, smears of sauce. Slowly the remains moved. Bread crusts fused into loaves, bones fleshed themselves whole and liquids drew together in bowls. By the time residents entered the tables were set with meals untouched.

Asha kept her expression calm. Her voice carried command even as unease gnawed beneath it. "How do your systems sustain this?"

Kael's reply was flat and almost indifferent. "They do not sustain. They are."

Later, Leon tested the phenomenon for himself. He dropped a cracked panel to the floor. It broke then rose in fragments and rejoined before his eyes. He turned it over twice, searching for flaws, then set it down sharply. "Effect before cause," he muttered. "The world turned inside out."

Imogen wandered to a group of residents gathered nearby. A young girl approached her and tugged at her sleeve. "Don't be sad about the end of our talk," the child whispered. Then, only after that, she smiled and asked, "What is your name?"

The words struck like a blow. Imogen sat frozen, notebook clutched in her hand, her heart racing with wonder and dread.

The silence was heavy back in their quarters. Asha paused at the doorway and rested her palm against the frame. "Stay alert," she said. "Here even the order of events cannot be trusted."

Leon set his handheld on the table. He checked it once more and repeated the figures aloud. "Entropy always increases," he muttered. "That is the rule. Forward is the rule."

Imogen sat on her bunk. She opened her notebook and looked at the child's face she had just drawn. The lines blurred, fading back into the paper. She closed the book with a snap and held it tight in her lap.

Station Janus carried on, serene in its reversals. The visitors felt their unease deepen with every breath.

.~.

Their quarters were small. Three bunks lined the walls. A narrow table stood between them and a port looked out onto a dim courtyard. The hum of hidden systems filled the silence. The three visitors sat for a while without speaking, each weighed down by thoughts too strange to voice.

Imogen broke first. She tapped her notebook with restless fingers then said, "It is not just the food or the tools. The people respond to us the wrong way round. They speak as though they already know what we will say."

Leon rubbed at his eyes. "I asked a farmer about nutrient cycles. He handed me a sheet of notes before I opened my mouth. For him, I had already asked." He gave a short laugh although there was no humour in it. "Conversations here run in reverse."

Asha Rey leaned against the table, arms folded, her eyes steady. "So you think their perception of time is different to ours. Explain."

Imogen hesitated but the pattern was clear. "They remember forwards. What we call the future is their past. What we call the past is blank to them as uncertain as tomorrow is to us."

Leon picked up a stylus from the table. He turned it between his fingers then dropped it. It rolled a little, then stopped. "So when I ask a question, it means nothing until it already belongs to their memory. Only then does it make sense." He gave a slow shake of the head. "We are walking against their current."

Imogen nodded. "That is why they answer before we ask. From their point of view, we already have."

The room fell quiet again. Asha's gaze sharpened. "Then how do they see us?"

Neither spoke until Imogen forced the words. "They see us leaving. From their side our departure has already taken place. Our arrival comes last."

The idea pressed heavily on all of them.

Leon leaned back, shaking his head. "So we are playing out a story where the ending is already known. We are just filling in the gaps." He let out a dry breath. "I prefer rules I can read straight."

Asha's mouth twitched, almost a smile. Her voice stayed firm. "Speculation does not change the facts. The present is all we share. That is where we can speak. That is where both timelines overlap."

Imogen pressed her notebook against her knees. Through the port she saw the courtyard. The children still played with their ball. It leapt into hands before leaving the thrower. Their laughter rippled through the air, light but out of step. She turned away quickly.

"Maybe certainty lies in different places," she said. "For us, the unknown is ahead. For them, it lies behind. Yesterday is their mystery."

Leon gave a short exhale, part sigh, part laugh. "That is philosophy not physics." He stopped there, unwilling to push further.

Asha rested one hand on the table, her fingers tapping once before stilling. "Whatever truth governs this place, ours remains. We observe. We endure. We hold fast to each other."

Neither Leon nor Imogen replied. The hum of the systems continued, steady and indifferent.

Outside, the courtyard lights dimmed. Children gathered their toys and drifted away. The port went dark.

Imogen did not open her notebook. She left it closed in her lap afraid the pages might erase themselves again.

.~.

Life in Janus revealed itself slowly. What seemed normal at first glance always held its opposite.

Director Kael allowed the visitors to attend a rite called a remembrance. The chamber was draped in pale cloth that stirred faintly in the recycled air. At the centre lay a figure wrapped in fresh linen, the fabric bright and unmarked. Around him stood friends and family, their faces calm.

Imogen felt a weight in her chest. She had known funerals before, but this was different. The mourners' voices were soft, yet they carried the tone of greeting rather than farewell. A child reached out to touch the shroud, curious rather than sorrowful. No one wept.

The same man appeared days later in the communal space. At first he was weak and moved with difficulty, as if illness were setting in. With time his steps grew steadier. The pallor left his face, his voice strengthened and his laugh grew louder. Finally he entered the birthing ward, welcomed with reverence.

Leon Ortega watched the process unfold. He spoke in a low voice. "Here, death comes first. Life unwinds from there."

He checked his wrist display but shut it down quickly, unwilling to see numbers that could not explain what his eyes confirmed.

Imogen had sketched the man during the remembrance. Later, when she looked back, the lines faded into the paper as though erased by time itself. She closed the notebook sharply, unwilling to see her own record come undone.

Asha Rey observed in silence. She noted the rhythm of relationships around them. Couples parted with warmth, then grew close, then finally met with shy smiles. Children clung to parents who, in time, seemed to forget them. From an outsider's view it looked tragic. Yet no grief showed in the residents. They carried themselves with serenity, as if symmetry itself was enough.

"Meaning does not depend on direction," Asha said to the others. "They live fully. The order is simply reversed."

Imogen shook her head. "They lose what matters most. They cannot build memory together. For them, discovery is always the ending, never the beginning."

Leon touched her shoulder briefly. "Maybe that is why they are calm. Their future is certain. It carries no fear."

That evening the three stood in the observation gallery. From above, they looked down on the library dome. Its shelves rose in curving tiers that bent gently inward. The pattern suggested a coil, subtle but unmistakable, as though knowledge itself was arranged in loops.

Imogen blinked and said nothing. She was unsure whether she had truly seen it or whether her mind had conjured order from strangeness. The image lingered all the same.

When they returned to their quarters, Asha paused at the doorway. "We keep to what we know," she said again firmly. "Don't forget that our work is to watch, to learn and to remain whole."

Leon gave a curt nod. Imogen sat with her notebook closed on her knees, unwilling to risk another drawing. Around them,

Station Janus continued as before, its people serene in a world where endings unfolded into beginnings.

.~.

The library occupied its own dome, vast and echoing. Light filtered through the roof panels in a dim shimmer, as though the sea above pressed its weight on the glass. The air was cool and carried a faint resonance that seemed to come from the walls themselves.

Shelves rose in concentric tiers, each lined with thin crystalline slates no larger than a hand. At a glance the place resembled a normal archive, orderly and calm. Only on closer approach did the differences reveal themselves.

Imogen lifted one of the slates. Its surface warmed to her touch. Words shimmered faintly in blue, settling into focus only when she looked directly at them. She realised with a shock that they were her own words, a fragment of a conversation she had not yet spoken. Her grip faltered and she set the slate down quickly.

Leon took another and examined it with care. "These are not histories," he said. "They are accounts of what is still to happen." He checked the symbols twice, repeating them under his breath. "Projections, not records."

Director Kael stood at the edge of the aisle. Her expression did not change. "The archive is complete," she said. "Everything that matters is remembered."

Asha Rey did not reach for a slate at once. She studied the tiers, her eyes running over the shelves. Her voice was steady. "Remembered in which direction?"

"In the direction that matters," Kael replied.

The answer admitted nothing and closed nothing.

Leon moved further along the aisle. He pulled another slate, then gave a short, strained laugh. "It is my handwriting. Notes on reactor coils. Exact phrasing I have not written yet. They already hold it as memory." He replaced the slate with more force than he intended.

Imogen could not look away from the shelves. "So for them, tomorrow is fixed," she said softly. "Their certainty lies where our questions begin."

Asha studied the tiers of crystal. "Unless they once lived forward as we do, before the collapse turned the flow. If that life was real, the memory of it has gone."

Asha reached for one of the central slates at last. Its surface glowed in her hands, the script forming into sharp clarity. She read aloud.

"Departure confirmed. Visitors puzzled but unharmed."

She set the slate back carefully. Her hand trembled though her voice stayed even.

Imogen turned to her quickly. "So they already know we leave. That we change nothing."

Asha tapped her finger once against her thigh, then let her arm fall. "Knowing is not deciding," she said. "Not for us."

Leon exhaled, almost a laugh, but bitter. "Then every move we make is already in their past. We are just repeating a script."

The three of them stood in silence. Around them the shelves glowed faintly. The curves of the tiers seemed to coil as they rose, subtle but undeniable. Imogen blinked, unsure whether she truly saw the pattern or whether her mind forced it into being. The image lingered as they turned away.

Asha spoke with quiet firmness. "Speculation will not help us. We observe, we endure, and we leave on our own terms."

Kael inclined her head. It felt less like agreement and more like recognition of words already spoken.

The visitors followed her out, their footsteps echoing in the dome. Behind them the crystals pulsed softly, recording a future already lived.

.~.

Arlen found me more often than I found him. He was a teacher, though I never discovered what he taught. He looked no older than me, yet he carried himself with the calm of someone who had already lived a full life. Every time we spoke, I felt the weight of certainty in his voice.

Our first meeting left me unsettled.

"I am sorry for the quarrel," he said, with a faint smile.

I frowned. "What quarrel?"

"You will see." He let the words rest there, as if the matter was already settled.

The second time, I tried to make a joke about Leon's habit of checking everything twice. Before I reached the punchline, Arlen laughed. It was not cruel. He was laughing with me but from a moment I had not yet reached. My irritation faded quickly, replaced by something closer to tenderness.

We sat together in the library dome on more than one occasion. I could not bring myself to touch the crystals so I kept to my notebook. I drew the curve of the dome, the lamps above, sometimes even the angle of Arlen's face when he turned his head. Too often, though, the lines blurred and faded, as though memory itself was being undone. I closed the book quickly each time, unwilling to watch the drawings disappear.

He noticed. "It troubles you," he said gently.

"It unsettles me," I admitted. "Your world begins with endings. You meet people at the close of things and part when it is new. I do not know how you live that way."

"For us," he replied, "beginnings carry no grief. They are welcomes, not losses. We remember the richness not the absence."

I shook my head. "If every friendship dissolved into strangers, if every love ended in first meetings, I would find it unbearable."

He studied me with calm patience. "You see only in one direction. For us, the meaning lies in the whole pattern. We part then we meet. We forget then we discover. The symmetry is what matters."

I asked if he ever wondered what lay before the collapse. He only smiled, as if the thought meant nothing. If there had been a forward life, it was lost to him.

I wanted to argue but I could not. His certainty was unshakable.

One evening when the dome lights dimmed to blue, he reached out and touched my arm. The gesture was gentle, almost tentative, but it stopped me all the same.

"Do not grieve when we part Dr Vance," he said. His voice was quiet, his smile almost shy. "I will remember you fondly at the beginning."

I could not answer. My throat was too tight. I closed my notebook and held it against me as though it could keep me anchored in my own time.

He let his hand fall though his gaze stayed with me. For him our farewell was already complete. For me, it felt like the start of something I had only just begun to understand.

.~.

The tremors returned, stronger this time. Lights flickered along the ceiling, shadows jerking in time with the failing rhythm of the reactor buried deep below the ice. The visitors felt the shift in their bones.

Leon Ortega bent over the console, speaking the numbers as they appeared. "Output falling. Field coils unstable. Collapse imminent." He checked again, repeating the words as though doubling them might force the system to hold.

Asha Rey studied the schematic projected across the wall. Lines of power flow faltered and looped back on themselves. "How long?" she asked.

"Days, maybe less." Leon rubbed his eyes. "When it fails, the domes fracture. Pressure falls. Nothing here survives."

They carried the news to Director Kael. She listened with her usual composure, as though the words were a repetition of something already known.

"Yes," she said. "The reactor has failed. That is where we began."

Imogen Vance blinked. "Began?"

Kael inclined her head. "From the moment of collapse, our memories opened. Our lives unfolded in reverse, each step taking us further from the end. For you it lies ahead. For us it is already behind."

The visitors stared at her in silence.

Back in their quarters, Leon spread schematics across the table, lines of calculation crowding the screen. "If we bypass the auxiliaries, reinforce the stabilisers, we can stop the reactor from failing. Buy them decades, maybe more." His words came quickly, sharpened by desperation.

Asha did not move. She watched him for a long time before speaking. "If we prevent the failure, we prevent their lives. The collapse is their beginning. Without it, there is no memory, no history, no people."

Leon's stylus froze in his hand.

Imogen spoke softly, her gaze distant. "Their world is symmetrical. They rise from disaster, grow younger until they meet their first day. What we call death is for them a doorway. It is not ruin but creation."

Leon shook his head, refusing the thought. "You're saying we just let it happen? We stand back and watch hundreds die?"

"They are not dying," Asha said firmly. "They are living their span in the only order open to them. To intervene would erase that span completely. We would be saving nothing."

Leon pressed his palm flat to the table. "That isn't engineering. That's surrender."

Asha placed a hand on his shoulder, her touch brief but steady. "It is restraint. Sometimes command is knowing when not to act."

The hum of the station deepened. Another flicker ran through the lights. The people of Janus carried on their routines:

children laughing in the courtyards, families walking together, workers tending plants. Their faces held no fear. For them, the collapse was not a threat. It was the moment from which all else flowed.

Imogen stood at the port, watching the courtyard. She tried to imagine life moving back through itself, each parting a beginning, each end a door to what lay before. "They don't fear the end," she said. "Because for them, it is the start."

Asha turned to the others, her voice calm, decisive. "Then we respect that. We leave when the time comes, and we let their story complete its symmetry."

Leon closed the schematics with slow reluctance. His hand lingered on the dark screen as though he could still force the numbers to change. Then he withdrew it.

The silence in the room was heavy, but final. The choice had been made.

.~.

The time to leave came without ceremony. The people of Janus gathered in the central dome, not to mourn but to welcome. Faces shone with quiet expectancy. Voices carried warmth, as though the visitors were stepping into the station for the first time.

For the crew of the Hesper it was a farewell. For the residents it was an arrival.

Director Kael stood by the docking bay, her presence steady. She took Asha Rey's hand and repeated the same words she had spoken when they first met.

"We are relieved you have come."

This time Asha did not correct her. She held Kael's hand firmly. "We are grateful for your welcome." She hesitated, then added, "Perhaps you lived once as we do, before the collapse turned the arrow. Perhaps this is your second journey."

Kael's eyes were calm, unreadable. "If it was so, we cannot remember it. Only what lies ahead remains to us."

Leon Ortega moved through the capsule's systems with practiced calm. He spoke each line twice, the cadence of ritual as much as verification. "Trajectory stable. Lock secure. Still stable."

Imogen Vance lingered near the crowd. Arlen stepped forward, his expression gentle, his hand brushing her arm.

"Until we meet again," he said softly. "At the start."

Her throat tightened. She wanted to speak but the words would not come. He withdrew, his certainty unshaken.

The airlock sealed. The capsule lifted, leaving the domes to shrink below them. Through the viewport they glowed faintly in the dark sea of Enceladus — fragile, luminous, suspended in their paradox. For the visitors, the lights receded. For the colonists, they were just beginning to shine.

Back aboard the Hesper, silence held the crew. The data they carried would ignite argument for decades.

Asha broke the stillness. "Not everything needs fixing," she said. "Some things need seeing. Perhaps they lived two lives: one forward into collapse, one back into their beginnings. Two arcs joined at a single point."

Leon leaned back in his seat, eyes closed, no further protest left in him.

Imogen sat apart, notebook unopened in her lap. She thought of Arlen's laughter before her words, his apologies for quarrels not yet spoken, his hand steady on her arm. She thought of the symmetry that shaped his world — life born from collapse, endings folding into beginnings.

.~.

I should have been grieving, but I wasn't. What lingered was not sorrow but wonder. For Arlen, our story was still ahead. For me, it was already softening into memory.

Asha's thought stayed with me. Maybe they had lived forward once before the reactor catastrophe. Raising families, building homes, shaping the domes. Then the collapse came and the arrow turned. They lived again, unspooling into their first day. Two journeys bound together by one moment of fire.

Perhaps that is how it must be. Our lives move forward toward an end. Theirs moved back toward a beginning. Each path complete, each carrying its own symmetry.

And maybe, I thought, that is not such a bad way to see the world.

10.
INTERSTELLAR
ENIGMA

In 2017, astronomers spotted something that had never been seen before. A faint speck of light drifted across survey images, moving too fast to belong to the Solar System. Its orbit was hyperbolic. Whatever it was, it had come from interstellar space and was already heading out again.

The object was named 'Oumuamua, a Hawaiian word meaning "scout" or "messenger." It was the first known visitor between the stars. Measurements soon showed it was unlike any comet or asteroid. It was elongated, perhaps ten times longer than it was wide, and it tumbled in a complex motion. Stranger still, it accelerated slightly as it passed the Sun yet there was no visible gas or dust to drive it.

Ideas multiplied. Perhaps it was a fragment torn from a shattered world. Perhaps it was a comet with hidden jets too weak for our telescopes to see. Or perhaps sunlight was pushing on a surface lighter than anything we had imagined.

None of these answers was entirely convincing. 'Oumuamua

left behind only questions.

What if it was not a natural object at all? What if it was a relic, drifting through the dark, carrying the memory of another civilisation?

.~.

The survey ship Hesper floated above Enceladus. Its hull glinted faintly against the pale glow of Saturn. Plumes of ice burst from the moon's surface and drifted back down as frozen snow. Beyond, the rings arced across the black, silent and immense.

Commander Asha Rey stood at the forward console. Numbers streamed past on the display. Her face was calm but her shoulders carried the weight of the moment. This was their only chance. If they missed the burn, the object would slip into the dark and be gone forever.

Leon Ortega bent over his station. "Navigation solution confirmed. Burn parameters locked. Twenty-three minutes to ignition. Delta-v within half a percent." He turned briefly. "This is it. Our intercept with 'Oumuamua."

Asha gave a short nod. "That's all we need."

Imogen Vance sat back at the science desk with her eyes on Saturn's faint light shimmering across the viewport. "Strange to think of it," she said. "Something from another star wandering in and us close enough to catch it."

Leon gave a tight smile. "Close enough with three months of careful slingshots. Any slip now and we'd have been thrown wide." He tapped his screen. "This is precision stacked on precision."

"It feels fragile," Imogen murmured.

"It is," Asha said. She moved to the side window where the curve of Saturn filled the view. "But this may be the only interstellar body we ever encounter. Fragile or not, we're ready."

Silence stretched for a moment. The hum of the ship pressed into the pause.

Imogen spoke again, quieter now. "We don't even know what we're chasing. Rock, comet, debris, something else. It could be anything."

Leon glanced up. "That's the point."

Asha keyed the intercom. "All hands, prepare for primary burn. Lock stations."

Leon's eyes flicked to the figures again, checking each in turn. His mouth set into a line. "The curve of Saturn gives us the push but the margin is tight. If we falter, it's gone."

Asha met his gaze. "We won't falter."

Imogen rubbed her arm absently, watching the icy plumes rise and fall on Enceladus. They reached high, curled and vanished back into shadow. She wondered if their work would leave any more trace than those fountains of ice.

The countdown continued. Sixteen minutes. Fifteen. Each second carried them closer to the moment that would seal their course.

.~.

Three days after the burn the Hesper cleared Saturn's pull. The planet dwindled to a pale disc in the aft cameras and its rings became a thin sliver of light. The ship glided on in silence. The crew worked their shifts and waited.

The first sign of their quarry was faint. A pixel flickered where no star should be. At first the software marked it only as an anomaly. Then the smear lengthened into a streak. Soon the streak became something more distinct.

On the main display the object showed itself as a sliver of rock. It stretched across several blurred pixels and changed shape with every turn. Sunlight struck its sides in sudden flashes. The light came without rhythm and caught the eye like a broken signal.

Leon leaned closer to the feed. "Target acquired. Rotation period is seven point three hours. It's tumbling on at least two axes. I'll refine the model with more rotations."

Asha stood behind him, eyes fixed on the screen. "That is not what I expected."

Imogen moved nearer. She studied the grainy, red-tinged outline. Planes and edges gleamed as though cut by a blade. "Elongation is extreme. Ten to one, maybe more. Could be a fragment from a shattered planet. But..." She left the thought hanging.

Leon picked it up. "But it could be engineered." He tapped the spectrum plot. "Reflections don't fit the surface. The colour is carbon dust yet the light curve is jagged. If this were a comet we'd see gas. There's none. Still, it accelerates as though something pushes it."

Asha frowned. "Radiation pressure?"

"Possible," Leon said. "If the surface is unusually light. Or if there's a thin sheet we can't see. Or something else."

Imogen stayed fixed on the feed. "Edges like these are unexpected after such a long journey. Dust grains and cosmic rays should have softened them, at least a little. They haven't. That doesn't look random."

The hum of the ship filled the pause. No one answered her.

The fragment rolled across the screen, its sharp edges catching the light. Each flare looked like a flash of teeth.

Imogen's voice softened. "It doesn't feel like it belongs here. As if it crossed space for millennia and now we've found it by chance."

Leon muttered, "Try telling that to the newsfeeds. Half of

them already call 'Oumuamua a messenger."

His hands moved over the console, chasing models that refused to settle.

Asha kept her eyes on the view. The object turned slowly and indifferently to their presence. For the first time she wondered if they were the watchers or if something unseen was watching them.

.~.

Three weeks after first sighting, the Hesper reached the intercept corridor. The object remained a red splinter against the dark yet no longer seemed distant. Every readout on Leon's console showed closure as their speed fell from thirty kilometres per second toward the visitor's slow retreat from the Sun.

Leon's voice stayed steady. "Final burn sequence loaded. Once we start, we have twelve minutes to bring our relative velocity near zero."

Asha stood beside him watching the fuel balance. "We get one chance. No overshoot. No restart."

Imogen aligned the external cameras. "All systems recording. I want full spectra during the burn."

Engines lit with a deep vibration that shook the hull. A low growl rolled through the decks as the ship began to slow. Numbers raced down the screens. G-forces pressed against them.

Leon's hands moved over the controls. "Six minutes to completion. Coil temperature climbing."

"Hold them steady," Asha said.

Noise thickened until it felt solid. Heat rose through the floor plates. Imogen braced her boots and watched the cameras. The red streak sharpened into a spindle whose sides caught the sun in erratic flashes.

"Three minutes," Leon called. "Velocity delta within two percent."

Asha's knuckles whitened on the handrail. "Maintain until stable."

The burn dwindled to a rumble then died. The vibration eased. The ship drifted. Leon read his screen and let out a slow breath. "Relative velocity matched. Less than four metres per second difference."

Asha checked the figures. "Distance to target?"

"Thirty-two kilometres, closing very slowly." Leon's voice dropped. "We're pacing it."

They stood in sudden quiet. After weeks of travel, the stillness felt unreal.

Imogen turned to the forward viewport. The object moved there, black on black, turning with slow grace. Sunlight touched one side and it glowed dull copper before sliding back into shadow.

She whispered, "We're beside it. After all that chase we're keeping time with something from another star."

No one replied.

Asha studied the fuel balance. "We've spent eighty-seven percent of reserves. That leaves enough to reach the inner system and nothing more."

Leon nodded. "Then this is our window. We stay on course and work with what we have. If it changes speed we can't follow."

Asha shut the console. "Understood. We make this count."

They floated in perfect formation, two travellers from different worlds sliding together through the dark. No radio noise came from the object. No measurable field or trace of outgassing.

Imogen said softly, "It feels like it's waiting."

Leon adjusted focus. "Or it doesn't even know we're here."

Asha faced the viewport. "Either way we start the survey once the coils have cooled."

They waited while heat bled from the systems. Cameras followed the rotation. Reflections flared and vanished across its uneven face.

Hours passed before Asha spoke again. "Prepare the drones."

Leon answered with one word. "Ready."

Power rose from the bays beneath the hull where six drones stood poised for release.

Outside, the interstellar visitor turned in silence while the humans drifted beside it in borrowed light.

.~.

The drones left the Hesper in pairs. Each one flashed a faint pulse of blue light before drifting into the dark. Their engines were silent. Their trails invisible. Telemetry stayed crisp and steady.

"Formation nominal," Leon said. "Separation five hundred metres. Relative velocity under two centimetres per second. They're matching the object's spin."

Asha stood beside him. "Keep the rotation offset minimal. We don't want them drawn into a blind side."

"Understood."

The object filled half the screen. Its surface looked neither smooth nor fractured but an improbable mix of both. Broad panels ran along its length, joined by seams too straight for natural breakage. Finer ridges crossed the gaps. The material glowed a muted red yet parts flared silver as if polished from within.

Imogen leaned close to the display. "Flat planes that wide shouldn't survive ejection. Any normal rock would have spun apart. Even a frozen block would show random erosion."

Leon's tone stayed even. "Composition scan shows carbonaceous material with trace metals. Reflectivity is twenty times higher than predicted. Some sections behave like a mirror."

"Mirrors," Imogen murmured. "Or panels."

Asha folded her arms. "Keep mapping. I want surface detail at one-metre resolution."

The drones moved closer, small sparks circling a giant. LIDAR grids built layer on layer of wireframe until the hologram filled the cabin. The geometry looked too ordered for comfort. Long edges. Flat faces. Right-angled shadows where no natural stress line belonged.

Leon magnified one section. "There. That recess is twenty metres across. Depth unknown. Edges perfectly parallel."

Imogen studied the image. "That's not geology."

"Or maybe it is," Leon said. "We've never seen erosion under interstellar radiation. You can't say what counts as natural here."

Asha stayed silent. Her gaze held on the display as one drone drifted toward the recess.

"Drone Three approaching cavity," Leon said. "Range ten metres. Surface composition scan running."

Static burst across the feed.

"Signal drop," Leon muttered. "Adjusting antenna."

The image cleared. The drone rotated to align its sampling arm. Its shadow stretched across the red face.

"Contact in three seconds," Leon said. "Two. One."

The feed died.

No flicker. No burst of light. Just absence.

Asha straightened. "Telemetry?"

"None," Leon said. The calm had gone from his voice. "No debris. No return echo. It's as if it never touched."

Imogen leaned over her console. "Could be a fault. Power surge. Static discharge."

"Or an active field," Leon said. "Something that reacts to proximity."

Asha looked between them. "We'll confirm before we assume. Send the next drone in from a different vector. Keep the arm retracted until final approach."

Leon hesitated then keyed the command. "Drone Four moving in."

On the display the tiny shape drifted toward the surface. Telemetry stayed steady until the final alignment. Then it vanished.

Imogen whispered, "That's no malfunction."

Asha's tone hardened. "Hold position. Recall the rest. No more contact attempts until we know what happened."

Leon's eyes fixed on the dark patch where the drones had gone. "Whatever did that leaves nothing behind."

Silence filled the room. The hologram kept turning, flawless and indifferent. Flat planes caught sunlight and flared like warnings across the void.

Imogen spoke softly. "If it reacts to being touched it knows we're here."

Asha said nothing. She faced the viewport where the object drifted beside them, immense and unmoved, as if listening.

.~.

The remaining drones circled at cautious distance. They moved in slow arcs with sensors fixed on the surface while the Hesper drifted beside them. No one spoke. The loss of the two probes had left a silence heavier than any void.

"Resume wide scan," Asha said. "Low power. Passive only."

Leon entered the command. Displays brightened with grids and pale outlines. Radar swept the object from end to end layer by layer. Gravimetric traces rippled across the graphs.

Imogen watched the lines settle. "Uneven mass. See the drop across the midsection."

Leon magnified the data. "Centres of inertia don't match geometry. Cavities, maybe tunnels. Large ones."

"How large?" Asha asked.

"Hundreds of metres. Some run parallel. Others twist like veins. Mass deficit close to ten percent."

Imogen frowned. "Empty space. Maybe ice pockets that vented away. Maybe not."

Asha studied the image. "The lines look too clean. Nature drifts toward chaos."

Leon shook his head. "Chaos can make symmetry. Crystals, fractures, long stress fractures under constant pressure. It can mimic design."

"Or design can mimic erosion," Imogen said.

They waited while the scan completed. The hologram formed a cross-section above the console. Inside the narrow body ran long corridors of nothing.

Imogen spoke first. "There's order in that pattern. The voids repeat at regular intervals. Ratios stay close to whole numbers."

Leon looked across at her. "Numbers don't prove intent. They only prove coincidence."

"Coincidence doesn't hold ratios," she said.

Asha let the words pass. "We have no proof either way. What matters is what we do next. We need readings from inside. Remote if possible."

Leon hesitated. "We can launch micro-probes from the remaining drones. They'll skim the cavities and return echoes. Any direct contact could trigger what destroyed the others."

Imogen nodded. "Then we avoid contact. Only scans. LIDAR and low-power radar. No arms. No discharge."

Asha nodded. "Do it."

Commands went out. Tiny icons slid across the screen toward the shadowed recesses. Their signals returned slow but clear. Patterns deepened. The inner map sharpened. Smooth planes replaced the jagged forms they expected from fractured rock.

Leon studied the image. "Those aren't random voids. The walls are planar within centimetres."

Imogen's tone hardened. "Natural processes don't shape planes like that."

Asha leaned forward. "If we assume intent what purpose fits that geometry?"

Leon shrugged. "Mass reduction, internal resonance, or something beyond us."

"Then we stop pretending we understand," Asha said.

They watched in silence as the last probe finished its pass. The map hung before them, a lattice of hollows inside a tumbling body of red metal and ice.

Imogen spoke softly. "Whatever made that pattern didn't leave it to chance."

Asha gave no answer. The object drifted beside them, vast and mute, its hidden cavities turning like lungs that refused to breathe.

.~.

The Hesper held station for nearly a full day. Its sensors gathered data while the crew moved through a rhythm of fatigue and fascination. Yet the balance was fragile. The object's slow tumble had begun to pull their orbit off line. The ship drifted toward one of the large cavities they had mapped before.

Leon broke the quiet. "Relative motion increasing. We're sliding inward."

Asha moved to the console. "Cause?"

"Microgravity gradient from its rotation. Our offset isn't stable."

"Can thrusters correct it?"

"Not enough. We'll need a short burn to re-align."

Imogen turned from her screen. "The coils aren't cooled. If we light them now they'll spike again."

Asha's answer came at once. "Then make it brief. We can't risk collision."

Leon keyed in the sequence. "Ten seconds should do it. Any longer and we burn through the shielding."

Asha nodded. "Do it."

Warning lights shifted from white to amber. The hum beneath them rose to a roar. The deck began to tremble.

"Five seconds," Leon said.

The sound thickened until it felt alive inside their skulls. Imogen gripped her station yet a jolt threw her sideways. She struck the wall with her shoulder and slid to the deck.

"Cut burn," Asha ordered.

Engines fell silent. The ship steadied into drift.

Imogen pushed herself upright. Pain ran down her arm. "I'm all right," she said though her voice betrayed her.

Asha knelt beside her. "You're not."

"It's a bruise. Nothing worse." She flexed her hand and winced. "Just help me up."

Leon turned from the readings. "Trajectory stable. We're back in sync. Coil efficiency down fifteen percent."

Asha lifted Imogen to her feet. "Can we compensate?"

"Maybe, but not for long. Every correction now costs double."

Imogen sank into a seat. "Then no more corrections unless we must."

The lights softened to white. The hum thinned to silence.

Asha looked through the viewport. The object rotated beside them, immense and close enough for detail. Sunlight slid across its facets in dull glints that flashed like distant fires.

Imogen followed her gaze. "It looks alive from here."

Leon shook his head. "Alive things move with intent. That just turns."

"Then intent may hide inside," she said.

Asha stayed on the view. "Whatever is inside, we don't chase it. Not until the coils cool and the hull checks out."

Leon gave a tired nod. "We're still getting clean data. I'll monitor drift. You should both rest."

Imogen smiled faintly. "Rest beside a thing that eats drones? Unlikely."

"Try," Asha said.

They stayed at their posts a while longer, listening to the soft tick of the systems. Outside, the interstellar body turned on its axis, each revolution slow enough to count yet steady as time itself.

.~.

'Oumuamua drifted beside them, slow and vast. Each turn of its body moved with a rhythm like a pulse. The drones hovered at range with their lights faint in the dark. Inside the Hesper, the crew watched the hollow map turning above the console. It showed a red lattice of tunnels and voids that had no right to exist inside a rock.

Leon leaned forward with his eyes fixed on the data. "We have range for one more sequence. The remaining drones still hold fuel and charge. If we send them in we can map the cavities directly."

Imogen sat with her injured arm held close. "Two are already gone. We still don't know what happened."

"That's why we need this run," Leon said. "If we hold back now we return with guesses."

Asha stood between them with her arms folded. "What's the risk?"

Leon paused. "Same as before. The cavities are wide but unstable. We could lose signal as they enter. There may be interference or debris. We can't tell which."

Imogen shook her head. "You call that risk? That's certainty. They'll vanish the same way."

Leon's voice stayed even but his jaw tightened. "They were built to fail if it meant discovery. That is their design."

"Discovery of what?" she said. "That something out here eats metal and silence?"

Asha raised a hand. "Enough. We plan this or we don't."

The argument faded into the hum of the instruments. Only the faint tick of cooling metal broke the stillness. Asha stepped closer to the hologram. The red outline turned until the largest cavity faced them like an open mouth.

"We send one," she said. "Single pass through the centre. Maximum data return. No second attempt if it fails."

Leon started to protest then stopped himself. He nodded once.

Imogen turned to him. "If it's destroyed that's our last chance."

He met her eyes. "Then at least we tried."

Asha gave the order. "Launch Drone Five."

The drone detached from the bay and drifted free. On the screen it shrank against the pale hull of the object before reappearing as a moving point. Telemetry stayed clean. The pulse of its signal kept time like a heartbeat.

"Entering cavity," Leon said.

Signal strength dipped, recovered, dipped again. Asha felt her own pulse match each drop.

"Still transmitting," Leon said quietly. "Depth one hundred metres. Two hundred. Structure smooth. No irregularities."

Static burst across the feed. For a breath the image froze. Then it cleared to reveal faint returns from deeper layers.

Imogen leaned forward. "There — reflection from the far side."

Leon checked the feed. "Multiple reflections. Metal density higher than before. Wait."

The signal spiked, flattened and died.

No flash. No echo.

Leon sat back with his mouth set hard. "Drone lost."

Asha said, "Confirm archive."

"Telemetry saved to buffer. Last packet intact."

"Display it."

The data unfolded as thin slices of colour across the screen. The returns showed lines beneath the cavity wall, shapes that repeated with impossible precision.

Imogen stared. "That's structure. It must be."

Leon looked uncertain. "Or noise from interference. There isn't enough to prove design."

Imogen pointed to one narrow band. "Regular spacing. Equal intervals. That's not random."

Asha studied the pattern. "It could be coincidence. Or it could mean we touched something built."

Silence returned.

Outside the viewport the red body turned with its slow indifferent grace. The lost drone was already gone.

Asha spoke at last. "We stop here. No more launches. We take what we have and head home."

Leon gave no protest. Imogen stayed silent.

The ship drifted beside the visitor from another star. Sensors kept running, questions kept growing.

Asha watched the object turn one final time and saw her reflection slide across its dark face. "We came this far," she said. "That will be enough."

.~.

The Hesper drifted clear of 'Oumuamua two days later. Its engines stayed cold while the coils cooled and diagnostics crawled through their cycles. When they finally lit the main drive the sound felt alien after so much silence.

We are turning home now. The object is shrinking behind us, a red sliver against the stars. I still glance at it on the aft display, waiting for movement that never comes.

My shoulder is healing. Asha says the bruise fades each day. Leon checks it whenever he finds a reason though he pretends he is reading stress lines in the hull. We are all doing the same thing really, watching small fractures and calling them data.

The strain between us has eased. There are still moments when quiet feels heavier than words yet we talk again. Asha speaks of repairs. Leon speaks of numbers. I try to understand what we found.

The last drone run keeps replaying in my mind. The feed went dark yet in that final instant it sent something real. Echoes that should not exist. Lines too straight for coincidence. Patterns that belonged to their own design. We cannot prove it was a structure but we cannot forget it either.

Maybe we touched something built. Maybe it was only matter shaped by time. It hardly matters now. The line between intent and accident blurred the moment we reached it.

The ship runs steady. Coils sit back within limits. We will reach the inner system in six weeks if nothing else fails. Asha hides her worry behind calm tone. Leon hides his behind data. I take my turn at the viewport.

The red glint fades a little more each hour. Part of me hopes it stays silent forever. Another part hopes it remembers.

We risked six drones, a ship and our nerves. For what? For a few traces of information and a question that refuses to die. Yet I think it was worth it. We came close to something not meant for us and lived to tell it. That is enough.

Maybe someone will chase it again one day when they have better drives and steadier hands. They might learn more. Or they might find the same silence waiting.

Until then we carry the questions home.

11. SINGULARITY BOUND

Black holes are usually imagined as cosmic predators that devour anything that strays too close. Yet theory shows they are not entirely silent. In the 1970s Stephen Hawking demonstrated that black holes radiate energy through quantum effects at the event horizon. For large black holes this emission is vanishingly small. But for tiny primordial ones, relics from the universe's first seconds, the radiation could be immense. Such objects would be smaller than atoms but weigh billions of tonnes. As they evaporate their output rises until the final instant. At that moment they release a burst of gamma rays and vanish.

No such relic has ever been confirmed. They may not exist at all. But if one passed near enough, humanity might try to harness its power. Careful feeding could turn it into a miniature star and drive entire colonies. Mishandling could unleash the most destructive weapon ever built.

The physics allows either path. The real question is whether humanity would choose wisely.

.~.

D r Amara Kade leaned closer to the console. The gamma-ray detector on SentinelNet-3 had just recorded a spike. Forty-one mega-electron-volts (41 MeV), lasting less than three milliseconds. The trace was sharp and balanced not the messy signature of background noise.

She called to Rajesh Iqbal, who was working two desks away. "Look at this. The spectrum is too precise."

Rajesh pushed his chair over and studied the screen. His brow furrowed. "It's not a pulsar. It isn't a flare either. Are you suggesting it's local?"

Amara nodded. Her throat was dry but her voice stayed even. "Yes. We may have just seen a primordial black hole finishing its evaporation."

Rajesh let out a low whistle. "A Hawking ghost. Half a trillion kilograms of compressed vacuum leaking away in gamma rays. You're serious?"

She did not answer straight away. The data still ran across her mind in waves of doubt and confirmation. Yet the pattern was there. A relic of the earliest universe revealing itself for a heartbeat. "Yes. I'm serious."

The term *primordial black hole* had been debated for decades. These objects, if they existed, were formed from density ripples in the first fractions of a second after the Big Bang. Too small to be seen by light, they could only be inferred by their faint Hawking radiation. Most would have vanished long ago. A few might still linger waiting to be noticed.

Rajesh rubbed his forehead. "Do you know what this means? If we can track it, if we can keep it from evaporating, we're looking at a controlled source of Hawking radiation. Free energy."

His voice carried both awe and unease. Amara felt the same pull. The discovery was not just scientific but practical, even dangerous. A black hole that could fit in the palm of her hand, yet release power greater than cities could consume.

She glanced again at the spectrum. Perfect symmetry. No

noise. No doubt. It had lasted for only milliseconds, but that was enough. They would be able to triangulate its position with follow-up detections.

For the rest of the shift she kept scanning. The signal did not repeat but that no longer mattered. It was already on its way to the central database. From there it would reach the desks of policy advisers, military analysts and research leaders. Amara knew the chain. Data never stayed in one place for long.

Later, walking back through the dim corridors of the research centre, she caught herself replaying the moment. One spike on a console had turned theory into reality. It would pull the attention of the world. Astronomers would argue, governments would posture, engineers would dream.

She wondered who would be trusted to go near such a relic if anyone at all.

.~.

Two weeks later, the European Space Operations Centre in Darmstadt had been transformed into a war room. Every seat in the main hall was filled. Flags of agencies and nations lined the walls and a ring of display screens floated above the delegates, each showing the same faint trace – the signal that Amara had first seen.

The room buzzed with voices in dozens of languages. Some were urgent but others were hushed and conspiratorial. A relic from the first seconds of the universe had been found and no one wanted to lose their chance to shape what came next.

At the podium stood Dr Rowan Pritchard. He had been drawn out of semi-retirement the moment the data was confirmed. His hair was greyer now than it had been during his last posting at Cambridge but his voice carried the same steady authority. He tapped the control panel and the hall fell silent.

"The object lies within five hundredths of an astronomical unit," he said. The holographic map lit up with a small red marker drifting against a field of stars. "That's roughly seven and a half million kilometres from Earth. Near enough to reach. Near enough to use."

General Naomi Roth, chair of the UN Space Security Council, leaned forward in her seat. "And the risks?"

Rowan adjusted his glasses. "Containable, if handled correctly. The mass is small enough to stabilise with the right systems. The radiation output is predictable. We are not speaking of a planetary body but of a relic smaller than an atom."

Naomi's voice carried a sceptical edge. "You are asking us to believe this can be contained."

Amara rose from her place among the scientific advisors. She had been asked to present her analysis and she felt every eye turn toward her.

"It can," she said. "If we feed it carefully, the output can be stabilised. Hawking radiation is continuous, not explosive, provided the black hole does not starve. That radiation can be collected and used. What we are discussing is not a danger by default. It is a potential source of continuous power."

Naomi narrowed her eyes. "Or a weapon."

"That is true," Rowan replied before Amara could answer. His tone was calm but there was no softening of the words. "That is why this cannot be handled by a single nation. It must be international, regulated and transparent."

A voice from the back of the hall cut in. "How long before it vanishes? How long do we have?"

Rowan touched the console again. A second display appeared, showing the predicted curve of Hawking radiation over time. "Months, at most. Perhaps less. Without intervention it will fade and release one final flash. We have one chance to reach it, stabilise it and test the concept of capture."

The arguments swelled. Engineers leaned across desks, sketching ideas on tablets. Policy experts whispered into headsets. Delegates from rival powers exchanged guarded looks.

Amara sat down again, her hands folded tightly in her lap. She knew what she had unleashed. The detection had not just been science. It had become a catalyst. A new form of energy dangled before humanity like fruit from a branch and every nation wanted to decide who would taste it first.

Later, in a smaller briefing room, the chosen core team gathered for the first time. Commander Juno Park sat at the head of the table, her expression sharp but composed. Beside her was Luka Marković, restless fingers already tapping at a datapad. Across from them Clara Weiss adjusted her glasses, her notes stacked in meticulous order. Amara found herself seated beside Rowan.

Rowan glanced at the others before speaking. "This mission will not be simple. We are not explorers chasing an object. We are stewards of something ancient. If it is captured it must be treated with the care one gives to a living system."

Luka gave a short laugh. "Living? It's a hole in spacetime not a plant."

Rowan's smile was faint but firm. "You will find that words matter. If you think of it as a tool, you will rush. If you think of it as prey, you will try to trap it. If you think of it as a partner, you may just give it the patience it demands."

Juno leaned forward. "The world has already decided. The mission is approved. Our job is to make it possible."

Amara felt the weight of the moment settle over her. The data she had first seen in silence would now propel a spacecraft into deep space. Engineers would design, pilots would fly and scientists would learn. But it would all come down to whether humanity could guide a speck of compressed spacetime without destroying itself.

She looked at Rowan who was already sketching trajectories in the air with his hands. He seemed composed and even serene. Yet she wondered how much strain the coming months would place on him.

.~.

I had not expected to stand at the heart of another mission. At my age I should have been shaping theories from the safety of libraries not planning an expedition to hold a fragment of the universe in our grasp. Yet the signal had changed everything. No one could ignore it and no one trusted the other to act alone.

The selection process took place in rooms that smelled of recycled air and quiet tension. Every candidate knew the weight of the work though few admitted it out loud. I watched the faces as they entered. Some showed hunger, others fear, most a mix of both. I carried their files in my head but I needed to see how they moved and especially how they listened.

Commander Juno Park was the first. She had flown supply craft to Mars during the early days of colonisation and had earned a reputation for discipline. Her answers were direct. No wasted words, no hedging. She met my eyes without challenge, but also without deference. Leadership is often about tone more than command and she carried the tone of someone who expected to be obeyed.

Next came Luka Marković. He could not keep still even while waiting to speak. His fingers traced patterns across the table, drawing invisible schematics. When I asked how he would stabilise a black hole's orbit he launched into three ideas before I had finished the question. He spoke too quickly but his mind was a furnace. Resourceful, reckless and brilliant in ways that needed a steadying hand.

Dr Amara Kade I already knew. Her data had brought us here. She was young compared to me but carried herself with the gravity of someone who had glimpsed what others only theorised. She checked her notes more than once, recalculating even when there was no need. That habit would serve her well. She had a careful mind though I sensed how deeply she wanted to see the relic with her own eyes.

Finally, Clara Weiss entered. A student of mine from Cambridge days, though she had long since stepped out from my shadow. She carried notebooks covered in neat symbols, and their margins filled with thoughts that ran beyond equations. Clara was analytical, yes, but also open to patterns others overlooked. I trusted her judgement although I worried how she would cope with the scale of responsibility.

As I watched them together, I realised the balance was fragile. Juno brought discipline, Luka brought energy, Amara brought caution and Clara brought insight. My role would not be to command them. It would be to hold them steady and to remind them that what we faced was neither experiment nor weapon but a relic of creation itself.

In the evenings I returned to my quarters and reviewed the mission outline. The craft would be small, a narrow frame of composite wrapped around ion drives and fusion boosters. Instruments would track the radiation output, mass drivers would feed the black hole fragments of matter and plasma shells would fine-tune its orbit. Everything depended on precision. A single miscalculation could tip stability into catastrophe.

I thought often about the object itself. A black hole with a mass of half a trillion kilograms, compacted into a sphere smaller than a proton. Invisible to the eye, yet heavy enough to bend trajectories across thousands of kilometres. It would be a ghost, detectable only through its whisper of radiation. To hold such a thing was both folly and promise.

I should have felt excitement, but instead I felt the weight of responsibility. Too many in the conference hall had spoken of energy grids, power markets or military leverage. Few had spoken of stewardship. To capture a singularity was not conquest. It was negotiation with the fabric of reality.

The team was confirmed within a week. We gathered in the hangar that would house the Vigilant. She stood waiting like a dart, slim and sharp, bristling with antennas and thrusters. Juno walked the length of the hull with the calm of a pilot already rehearsing her commands. Luka circled the mass drivers, muttering to himself about redundancies and contingencies. Amara ran her hand across the instrument panel as if it were a living thing. Clara stood apart, taking notes in silence.

I spoke to them before launch preparations began. "We are not just explorers. We are caretakers of something old and dangerous. Do not think of it as a resource. Think of it as a companion that will test our patience. If we treat it with care, it may endure long enough to change the future."

They listened, though each absorbed the words differently. Juno nodded once, steady as ever. Luka looked impatient, eager to begin. Amara's eyes shone with resolve. Clara's pencil moved as she underlined the word *companion*.

Later, alone, I allowed myself a brief smile. They were young but they were capable. I wondered if I had been brought along to guide them or if my real task was to see whether humanity itself was ready for what it was about to hold.

.~.

The Vigilant rose from Kourou on a column of fire and plasma. For a moment it seemed fragile against the sky, a needle of alloy and composites pressed upward by engines older than its mission. Amara watched from the crew cabin as the horizon fell away and the Earth curved beneath them. She tried to hold the image steady, knowing that once they were clear of orbit the planet would become nothing more than a blue point.

Commander Juno Park sat forward in her harness with her hands resting on the controls though the ascent was fully automated. She checked the displays with a calm eye, not because she distrusted the software but because the act of watching anchored her. Luka Marković muttered calculations under his breath and scribbled figures on his slate even as acceleration pressed him into his seat. Clara Weiss closed her eyes, lips moving silently as if rehearsing equations. Rowan Pritchard leaned back, still and quiet, conserving energy for what lay ahead.

The ship settled into a quietly curving trajectory towards

its destination. A soft vibration ran through the cabin, a continuous thrum that would carry them for weeks.

"Trajectory confirmed," Juno said. Her voice was level, clipped, but carried the relief of clean numbers. "Thirty-six days until rendezvous."

Luka exhaled sharply. "Thirty-six days staring at a point smaller than an atom."

Amara gave a small smile. "Perspective is everything. It is the smallest thing we have ever chased, and it may become the largest gift."

Rowan opened one eye. "Or the sharpest test."

No one answered. The silence carried them out of Earth's shadow.

The transit blurred into a rhythm of routines. Instruments were calibrated and recalibrated. Mass drivers were cycled through test firings, ejecting fragments of rock held in sealed chambers. Plasma fields were mapped in simulations. Amara ran her hands over every dataset, checking and cross-checking. Clara annotated her logs with layers of probability curves, her neat handwriting filling page after page. Luka adjusted thruster algorithms and then adjusted them again. Juno wrote nothing, spoke little, and carried the weight of command in the simple steadiness of her presence.

At meals the crew spoke in half-jokes. Luka described the black hole as a furnace waiting to be stoked. Clara corrected him, insisting it was more like a balance scale that would tip if they fed it too quickly. Juno listened and offered no metaphors. Rowan occasionally interjected with a dry observation that pulled a smile from Amara despite her nerves.

Weeks passed. The stars outside grew sharper as the Earth shrank into memory. The ship's sensors began to register faint fluctuations and minute shifts in the gravitational background. At first it was only noise, indistinguishable from instrument drift. Then the pattern began to cohere.

Amara leaned over the detector display. "There. That spike matches the initial trace."

Clara compared it against her simulations. "The curve is correct. This is it."

Juno adjusted their course by a fraction. The ship obeyed with a faint shudder. The crew held their breath.

The object itself could not be seen. The detectors ticked like a heartbeat, registering gamma rays that spread through the void. Gravimeters picked up ripples in the field, subtle but insistent. The black hole was hidden there yet undeniable.

Luka stared at the readouts. "Half a trillion kilos and I still can't feel it."

Amara shook her head. "The mass is concentrated but the influence spreads so far it dilutes before it reaches us. The only thing we can measure here is the radiation."

Rowan's voice was low, almost reverent. "A ghost of the universe waiting for us to guide it."

The Vigilant drifted closer. Each adjustment was logged with precision. Each pulse of the thrusters recorded in triplicate. There was no sense of scale, no looming shape ahead only numbers crawling across displays. Yet every number told the same story. They were approaching a relic born at the beginning of time.

When Amara finally unbuckled and floated through the cabin, she pressed her hand against the hull. Beyond that thin layer of metal and shielding the void stretched unbroken. Somewhere within it the object waited. She thought of her first glimpse of the signal on the console at home, a millisecond spike that had shaken the order of her life. Now it had become real, a destination instead of a question.

The others slept in shifts but Amara found little rest. Each time she closed her eyes she pictured the curve of radiation rising and falling. The knowledge that they were moving towards it filled her with both dread and wonder.

Rowan found her awake one cycle and sat with her in silence.

He did not offer advice. He simply rested his hand on the edge of the console and looked out at the black. For once she did not feel the need to speak either. The silence was enough.

.~.

The Vigilant's instruments fixed on the faint silhouette of Keel-One, an asteroid hastily selected as their shepherd once the black hole had revealed itself. In the weeks since detection its orbit had been nudged by remote tugs, just enough to bring it into a useful position. It was no more than a dark shape against the stars, turning slowly in the sunlight but its path offered the crew a chance. If they aligned it correctly Keel-One would serve as a gravitational anchor for the black hole.

Juno adjusted the thrusters with tiny pulses. The ship shifted almost imperceptibly, slipping into the corridor that had been mapped months before. Numbers flowed across the displays, each one checked and confirmed. Clara monitored the simulation output, tracing the predicted paths of the black hole once it drifted into Keel-One's sphere of influence.

Rowan stood near the main console, his hands folded behind his back. He watched the team work without interruption, though occasionally his finger lifted to point at a figure or correction. He did not need to say much. Presence carried its own command.

"This is not capture," he had reminded them during training. "It is persuasion. We are asking gravity to do the work for us."

Amara thought of those words as she entered another set of coordinates. The black hole was a ghost that responded only to mathematics. They could not touch it. They could only guide it, and even that required patience measured in days rather than seconds.

The first course correction took place over eighteen hours. Each thruster burn lasted no more than a few seconds, yet each one was logged and cross-checked. Juno's eyes never left the readouts. Luka complained about the slowness of the process but still made careful notes on the engine performance. Clara's pencil moved steadily across her notebook, the margin filled with new equations. Amara stayed quiet and focused on the detector curves that revealed the object's path.

At last the gravimeter registered the faintest pull toward Keel-One. The numbers edged upward. Amara allowed herself to exhale. "It's moving with us."

Luka leaned forward. "Still feels like we're trying to leash a ghost."

Clara shook her head. "Not leash. Balance. If the vectors hold, the object will fall into a stable orbit around the asteroid."

Rowan spoke then, his tone calm. "Gravity is our leash. Not chains, not force. A dance that requires both partners."

The manoeuvres continued for days. Each adjustment carried risk, though the ship itself never shuddered. All the drama lived in the numbers. The team ate, slept, and returned to their stations with the same fixed rhythm, each shift marked by another micro-burn or vector correction.

Juno kept her commands brief. "Fire thruster three, two seconds. Log confirmed. Align by one point five degrees." She spoke as if reciting from a script, yet her steadiness kept the others focused.

Luka's restlessness grew. "We could shorten the timeline with a heavier burn," he argued more than once.

Juno dismissed him with a shake of her head. "Patience holds the system. Hurry breaks it."

Rowan gave Luka a measured look. "Speed tempts but precision sustains. Remember which one history values."

By the end of the week the gravimeters stabilised. The black hole had settled into Keel-One's gravitational sphere. It drifted in an invisible loop, its presence marked only by the constant tick of radiation on the detectors. Clara confirmed the orbit against her simulations.

"It's holding," she said. "The path is stable."

Amara let her head fall back against the rest of her chair. For the first time since launch she allowed herself a moment of release. They had persuaded the universe to bend, not by force but by guidance.

Rowan gave a faint nod as though he had expected no other outcome. Yet Amara saw how his fingers lingered on the edge of the console as if drawing strength from its solidity. He had not spoken of his health and no one had pressed him but the lines on his face were sharper than she remembered from Cambridge.

Keel-One now carried two companions: the Vigilant circling at a cautious distance and the black hole drifting unseen in its gravity well. The stage was set for the next phase. Feeding would begin soon and with it the true test of whether humanity could live alongside a relic of the first moments of time.

Amara closed her eyes for a moment and imagined the view from far away. An asteroid tumbling through the void, a spacecraft looping nearby, and somewhere within the system a singularity too small to see but heavy enough to matter. A partnership had been formed. Fragile, tentative, and extraordinary.

.~.

The Vigilant's crew had rehearsed this stage a hundred times. Simulation after simulation had shown that a black hole could be sustained with steady feeding, each fragment of matter thrown across its invisible horizon like fuel into a furnace. Now they faced the real attempt.

Luka Marković checked the mass driver housings for the fifth time that day. He ran his hand along the feed rails, searching for anything loose. Juno Park watched him with an expression caught between patience and warning.

"We have checked every system," she said. "If you don't sit down soon, I'll strap you there."

Luka grinned but his hands lingered. "One jam at the wrong moment and we'll burn through months of planning."

Amara Kade stood at her station and monitored the detectors. "Radiation output is holding steady at two terawatts. Stable baseline."

Clara Weiss adjusted her glasses and studied the probability curves she had drawn in neat lines across her slate. "Feed rate begins at two kilograms per day. That should hold the curve flat."

Rowan listened in silence. He had already delivered his lecture during training. Feeding was not indulgence but balance. Too much and the singularity would flare uncontrollably. Too little and it would collapse. He watched the others now, his eyes sharp, his posture still.

Juno gave the order. "Prepare first feed."

Luka tapped a sequence into the controls. A fragment of asteroid rock, no larger than his fist, was loaded into the mass driver. The chamber sealed. The crew held their breath as the firing sequence initiated. A pulse of magnetic force hurled the fragment into space. Instruments tracked its trajectory until it vanished at the event horizon.

Amara called out the numbers. "Absorption confirmed. Gamma flux rising. Output steady."

The detectors hummed. A faint vibration ran through the ship, though the black hole itself remained invisible. Clara marked the reading with a clean line of ink.

"One successful feed," she said. "Radiation output consistent."

The process repeated through the next days. Tiny fragments were launched one by one. Each vanished into the void. Each left behind a measurable pulse of energy. The Vigilant's power systems began to draw from that radiation, converting it through magnetic channels into usable current.

Amara allowed herself a smile. "We are throwing pebbles into the dark and catching fire in return."

Rowan gave her a sidelong look. "Remember what fire can do if left untended."

The words settled over the crew. None argued.

By the third week, the system ran almost smoothly. The black hole drifted in orbit around Keel-One, its radiation steady, its feeding automated by Luka's careful programming. Amara began to relax her grip on the console. Juno allowed herself longer silences between checks. Clara filled her notebook with calculations that stretched into elegant patterns.

Then the alarm sounded.

The detectors spiked in a single violent surge. Radiation doubled, then tripled. The ship's lights dimmed as automatic shielding engaged.

"Flux at six terawatts," Amara shouted. "Climbing fast."

Luka's hands blurred across the console. "Feed sequence broken. Driver three jammed mid-cycle. The pellets are hitting out of rhythm."

Clara stared at the rising curve. "That's throwing the whole field unstable. The spectrum's uneven."

Juno's command came sharp and fast. "Emergency override. Force a correction feed. Bring it back on sequence."

Luka diverted power to the backup drivers. Fragments of Keel-One launched in stuttering bursts, each impact sending jagged pulses across the detectors. The readings shivered, dipped, then began to fall back toward safe bands.

Amara let out the breath she had been holding. "Stabilising. Output steadying at four terawatts."

The alarms quieted, but the silence that followed was heavier than before. The relic had shown them what happened when they lost the rhythm.

Rowan pressed a hand against the console. His voice was calm but Amara noticed how he drew breath between each phrase. "This is what I warned you of. The balance is fragile. We must not trust automation without vigilance."

Juno gave a single nod. "We stay on manual oversight. No exceptions."

The crew returned to their stations but the mood had shifted. Each pulse of the mass drivers carried weight now, each detector reading lingered longer on the screen.

That night-cycle Amara found Rowan in the quiet of the observation bay. He leaned against the rail, eyes fixed on the scatter of stars.

"You're pale," she said.

"I am older than the rest of you," he answered, not looking at her. "That is no secret. My body knows it even when I would prefer to ignore it."

She hesitated, then asked, "Should you be here?"

Rowan smiled faintly. "That is exactly why I should be here. To remind us all what we are holding."

He did not say more and she did not press him. The detectors ticked softly in the background. Each pulse a reminder that the relic still lived in their care.

.~.

The Vigilant had held steady for weeks. The detectors ticked with calm rhythm The orbit around Keel-One stayed clean and the plasma fields wrapped the relic in symmetry. Confidence began to creep into the days though no one spoke of it.

The warning came without mercy. The detectors shrieked across every console and the cabin drowned in red.

Amara shouted above the noise. "Radiation spike. Fourteen terawatts and climbing."

Clara's pen froze over her notebook. "The curve is unstable. If it holds like this, the orbit will shear loose."

Luka hammered his console. "The plasma fields are out of phase. Symmetry's gone."

Juno's command cut through us all. "Emergency stabilisation. Lock correction now."

My mind sharpened the way it always did when numbers turned hostile. The curve rose too fast. Probabilities folded into catastrophe before my eyes. I felt the ache in my chest but forced my voice to hold. "You must bring it back into rhythm. Do not fight it. Guide it."

Luka's hands blurred. Secondary field coils lit, pushing the balance back into place. Jagged pulses rattled the detectors then the curve began to dip.

Amara's voice trembled. "Stabilising. Output falling. Four terawatts and steady."

The alarms quieted. Silence weighed heavier than the noise. The relic had shown its teeth and for a moment it had seemed we might lose everything.

I pressed down on the console rail. My chest burned, breath ragged. I told myself it was strain but the truth had lived in my body for weeks.

Amara turned and saw my face. She started forward but I shook my head. "Stay at your station," I tried to say. My voice broke thin against the effort.

The pain sharpened and I looked at them one by one. Juno unflinching at her post. Luka staring at his readouts as though will alone could hold them steady. Amara's eyes filled with fear she could not hide. Clara's pencil still hanging useless in mid-air.

I wanted to tell them again of balance, of rhythm, of patience. The words caught. My chest heaved once, then again and no more.

Amara's hand gripped mine. I heard her whisper though I could not answer. The word that slipped through was the only one that mattered.

"Balance."

The rest fell away.

.~.

Amara felt the moment his hand slackened in hers. She whispered his name again, though she already knew. The cabin was silent except for the low hum of the detectors, steady now as if mocking the chaos that had just passed.

Clara dropped her pencil. It clattered against the deck with a brittle sound that seemed to echo too long. Luka sat back, his face pale and his eyes fixed on the console as though he could undo what had happened by refusing to look away. Juno remained at her post, her shoulders squared but her jaw was clenched tight.

No one spoke. The man who had anchored them, who had reminded them that this relic demanded patience rather than force, now lay still at their feet. Amara kept her hand on his a moment longer, unwilling to let go.

At last Juno broke the silence. Her voice was even but frayed at the edges. "He knew the risk. He came anyway. We will finish this mission because he would have wanted that."

They carried Rowan to the observation bay. The crew moved as if underwater. Each step slowed under the weight of grief. They wrapped him in the mission flag, a strip of deep blue embroidered with the emblem of the Vigilant. Juno read the words of committal in a clipped but steady tone. Luka stood stiff with his fists pressed tight at his sides. Clara's cheeks were wet and her glasses fogged. She did not look away..

Amara's hands shook as she keyed the release. The hatch opened and Rowan drifted out into the dark. For a moment his form glowed in the starlight then he was gone, carried into the same silence that now held their black hole.

No one moved. The relic pulsed in their instruments, balanced again, its hunger sated for the moment. It seemed cruel that it endured while Rowan did not.

In the days that followed, they worked with renewed discipline. No one questioned Juno's orders. Luka checked and rechecked every line of code. Clara filled her notebook with new calculations, her handwriting darker and sharper than before. Amara buried herself in the detector logs, unwilling to leave a single number unverified.

Rowan's absence became a presence of its own. His words

lingered in the cabin: balance, patience, rhythm. Each decision seemed to carry his voice reminding them not to push and not to force.

By the time the Vigilant disengaged six months after launch, the system was stable. The singularity circled Keel-One in a narrow orbit. The mass drivers fed it on schedule, the radiation flowed through magnetic fields into power collectors and the detectors ticked with calm precision. Humanity had leashed a relic from the first seconds of the universe.

Amara wrote the final entry in her log. She did not try to hide the tremor in her hand.

"We captured a ghost," she said aloud as she typed. "We fed it, we balanced it and it gave us power in return. But nothing about this belongs to us. We can guide it and use it but we remain guests. Rowan reminded us of that every day. His absence marks the cost of what we have done and his words will remain the measure of whether we deserve this gift."

She saved the entry and closed her slate. Outside the viewport Keel-One drifted on, carrying its invisible companion. For an instant she thought she saw movement, a faint distortion in the starlight. She pressed her hand against the glass and whispered the word Rowan had given them as his last.

"Balance."

12. ENTANGLED HEARTS

Quantum entanglement links two particles so that their states remain connected, no matter the distance between them. Measure one and the other responds instantly. A phenomenon Einstein once dismissed as "spooky action at a distance."

In reality, entanglement cannot send messages faster than light as the no-signalling theorem forbids it. But what if that limit could be bent? What if entangled pairs could carry not just correlations but meaning, voices, laughter and even love across four light-years? How would it change connection, control and the loneliness of a colony under alien skies?

.~.

Eira sat in the darkened chamber, palms flat on the console waiting for the lattice to hum. Only the vents whispered, a soft sigh against the dome's silence. The Aurora colony dome above was asleep. Thirty thousand souls dreaming under glass on Proxima b, the world circling the nearest star, Proxima Centauri. But she was awake and restless. The lattice needed her. Nobody else could do this work.

The chamber glowed faint blue. Threads of light spun in

the vacuum core, halves of entangled particles ferried across interstellar space in fragile capsules. Their twins remained in orbit around Mars, bound to these by physics itself. Each flicker reminded her: distance did not matter. What collapsed here collapsed there.

"Eira." The voice came, not through speakers, but inside the lattice itself.

She exhaled. "I'm here."

Kieran. His words arrived from Mars without delay. Four light-years crossed in less than a heartbeat. It always felt like speaking through glass: fragile, transparent, immediate.

"You're late."

"Recalibration," she said. "The colony grid's failing again."

"You always have an excuse."

"You always have complaints."

Silence pressed in but not emptiness. Truth lingered there. This was the only real-time bridge between two star systems. Officially, they relayed supply requests and mission logs. Unofficially, it had become something else.

The first time she heard him, she had laughed. Scientists warned it might feel unnatural, hearing speech tied to state collapses but his voice bloomed in her mind like a whisper at her shoulder. That ordinariness became addictive. Proxima b offered only copper skies, tar-black ice seas, storms that made the dome tremble as though ghosts rattled its shell. Kieran's voice was the one thing that felt alive.

Tonight, though, it was sharp.

"They're changing the supply runs."

Her chest tightened. "What do you mean?"

"The Directorate's rolling out new capsules. Beamed sails pushed at a third of a g, peaking at eighty per cent light-speed. They get here in eight years instead of forty. But they're small. Too small."

Eira frowned. "Smaller payloads mean fewer qubits."

"Exactly. We only ever get the halves shipped here and, with smaller loads, there aren't enough channels for everyone. The Directorate keeps the main lattice for themselves and their acolytes. The rest of us go back to light-speed relays. Four years each way, eight for a reply."

She saw it clearly: the council locked out, her console dead and his voice drifting beyond reach. "They'll cut us off."

"Yes." A pause. Then, softer: "Maybe that's why I like talking to you. Because I know it can end."

The words landed more dangerously than the storms outside. The Directorate recorded every session, flagged tone and inflection. Yet entanglement always produced noise. Gaps the logs missed. In those cracks they had built something fragile.

"You can't let them take this from us," she whispered.

.~.

Days blurred. Dust storms clawed the dome. Hydroponic towers faltered. Miners demanded power the farms could not spare. Eira patched, balanced and endured. Yet every shift she returned and waited for the lattice glow.

"I found a way," Kieran said one night.

He explained quickly. By skewing the collapse sequence they could carve private channels into the noise. Invisible to Directorate oversight.

Eira's pulse raced. "That's sabotage."

"That's survival. Once the new capsules arrive and the Directorate reallocates, we're out. Unless we write ourselves in before the cut."

She stared into the swirl of light. Physics insisted it was only probability and spin. Yet she swore it looked back, an eye blinking from four light-years away.

"What do you want to say, Kieran?"

A pause, then: "That I'd rather be there. With you."

The words hit harder than alarms. She had felt it in the laughter between reports, in the warmth slipping past static.

But never spoken.

"You don't know what it's like here," she said, voice shaking.

"I don't care. Distance doesn't matter. When we talk you feel closer than anyone else has ever been."

She pressed her hand against the cool glass as though he might press back.

.~.

Weeks later the announcement came: capsule turnover complete, allocation revised, civilian lattice access revoked. The council raged, fists pounding tables, voices rising. Eira barely heard them. She sat waiting for the hum, terrified it might be the last.

Kieran's voice came strained. "If we carve the channel, there's no going back. They'll know we tampered. Penalties are severe."

"And if we don't?"

"Then we wait eight years for every answer. We lose this."

Her throat tightened. She thought of the dome quivering in the storm, of the weight of four light-years pressing down, of his voice, the one thing that cut through the emptiness.

"I don't want to lose you," she said.

"Then we do it."

.~.

That night they rewrote the protocols. Rough and imperfect. Scratches carved into chaos with desperation and defiance. The lattice flickered with jagged light.

"Can you hear me?" Kieran asked.

"Yes."

"No logs. No monitors. Just us."

His voice was unshackled and free. Eira laughed, the sound spilling into the lattice and rippling outwards. For a moment the distance collapsed. Not Proxima. Not Mars. Not the Directorate. Just two entangled voices bound across the void.

The next morning the Directorate's channel lists showed Proxima silent. To the colonists, the solar system seemed farther away than ever.

But in a quiet chamber beneath the dome, the console still glowed with secret light.

Eira leaned close.

"Good morning," he said.

She smiled across four light-years.

13. QUANTUM BEADS

At the quantum scale, the world refuses to behave as common sense expects. Particles can exist in more than one place at a time, spin in opposite directions simultaneously or become mysteriously linked across distance. This is superposition and entanglement. The strangeness at the heart of modern physics. In our everyday world such effects vanish, washed out by scale and noise, leaving us with a reality that appears stable, definite and predictable.

But what if quantum rules did not fade so easily? What if objects visible to the eye and tangible to the hand could remain in superposition. Shimmering in several places at once until observed? What would it mean to handle matter that is both here and not here, responsive to every gaze? And how would people live with the knowledge that reality itself waits for them to decide which version of it exists?

.~.

In the synthesis chamber of Enceladus Orbital Colony Gamma-3, silence was not the absence of sound but the presence of control. Every vibration, every stray photon, every whiff of thermal noise was damped away, leaving only the steady pulse of containment fields. Inside the glass-walled chamber a handful of translucent spheres shimmered faintly. They were small enough to be mistaken for dust yet each one represented a step across the threshold of possibility.

Dr Clara Weiss stood alone, her posture taut. For years she had modelled the mathematics of quantum coherence, sketching impossible lattices and calculating half-lives of states that should never last. At last the engineers had delivered the material she had designed/ Aetherium, grown atom by atom in the vacuum furnace, latticed into stability like a crystal tuned to the rules of probability itself.

Two millimetres across. Stable for minutes at a time. Macroscopic objects that behaved like electrons in a double-slit. She typed a brief note into the colony's comm system.

Subject: Initial batch successful. Requesting assistance.

To: Tamsin Harlow, Engineering Division.

Clara's lips tightened as she pressed send. Tamsin was brilliant, no one denied that, but she was also impulsive. Forever chasing the next anomaly or the next loophole in the laws of nature. Clara needed her energy but she also feared it. Still, if anyone could push the beads beyond theory, it was Tamsin.

The chamber lights dimmed automatically as the beads stabilised. They glowed faintly as if aware of the attention they were about to receive.

Outside, Enceladus spun in silence, its icy surface reflecting the pale light of Saturn. Humanity had learned to live here on the edge of the possible. Now, with these beads, they might learn to bend possibility itself.

.~.

I never get tired of the walk out to the lab. The main habitat is all bustle. Voices in the corridors, hydroponic gardens humming and recycled air tinged with cooking oils. But step through the transfer lock and the world changes. The gravity fades, the air tastes sharper and the only sound is the faint creak of the tether spine holding the lab to the rest of the colony.

Most people don't like making the trip. They say it feels exposed with all that blackness pressing against the viewport and only Enceladus glittering below. But I love it. Out here I can almost believe the universe is waiting to whisper its secrets if I dare lean close enough.

Clara had called me specifically. That's unusual. She normally works alone, polishing equations until they gleam and refusing to let anyone smudge the surface. We've crossed paths before. She's precise to a fault, I'm... well, not. But somehow we work together. She steadies me and I make her loosen her grip on certainty if only by a fraction.

As I floated down the spine I wondered what could tempt her to send for me. The message was terse: *Initial batch successful. Report to lab.* No details, no hints. Just that measured Weiss tone.

The lab module emerged from the dark, its surface bristling with cooling vanes. I cycled through the airlock and let the gentle hum of cryogenics wash over me. The temperature was colder here, deliberately so. Even before I reached the central bench I knew something delicate was being sheltered.

Clara was at the console, as upright and self-contained as ever. She didn't look up immediately; her hands moved in swift arcs across a holographic display, adjusting containment parameters. Only when the door sealed behind me did she nod. "Morning, Tamsin. You're just in time."

On the bench lay a tray. For a second I thought she was teasing me with a handful of glass marbles. Each sphere was only two or three millimetres across. Ordinary. Dull. I nearly laughed.

Then I saw it. A faint shimmer, like moonlight caught in water, flickering not quite in step with my eyes. The beads seemed to hesitate between being solid and not, as if the air couldn't decide whether to hold them.

"These are them?" I whispered.

Clara allowed herself the tiniest smile. "The first aetherium quantum beads. Until observed, each one exists in every possible state at once. Position, spin and vibration are all undefined until you look."

I reached instinctively towards the tray. She shot me a look sharp enough to freeze my fingers. "Careful. Even a stray photon will do. One careless glance and a bead could collapse somewhere inconvenient."

"Inconvenient?" I grinned, trying to break her sternness. "That's one way of saying it."

She didn't return the smile. Her caution wrapped the room tighter than the containment fields. But the beads themselves didn't care. They glowed softly daring me to meet them.

I pulled back my hand reluctantly but inside my pulse drummed. This wasn't just another experiment. It wasn't even just Clara's breakthrough. This was a conversation with reality itself and I was ready to start speaking.

.~.

The lab felt different once the tray of beads had been placed under the main lights. Every hum, every click of the cooling systems seemed sharper, as though the room itself waited.

Clara adjusted the photon shields and then stood back. "We'll begin with a simple test. Use these." She held out a pair of ceramic tweezers.

Tamsin turned them in her hand. "Do they always look so ordinary?"

"They are ordinary in shape. Not in behaviour. Approach slowly. Let the instruments catch the projections."

Tamsin leaned closer to the tray. The beads flickered with edges soft as though they refused to settle. The display above the bench lit up. Dozens of faint images scattered across the field, each one a possible location.

"Feels like they're waiting for me," she murmured.

"They're not waiting," Clara said. "They are in every place at once. Your presence will decide which remains."

The projections snapped. A single bead rested near the edge of the tray.

Tamsin held her breath and pinched it between the tweezers. The weight was almost nothing. Yet she felt the pressure of a faint resistance like the bead wanted to slide out of her grip. "It's solid. But not. Do you feel that?"

"I see the readings. Photons, a small thermal spike, a ripple in the containment field. Nothing mystical."

Tamsin rolled her eyes. "You really know how to kill wonder."

Clara glanced at her with an unreadable expression. "Wonder doesn't protect the sample. Control does."

They worked in a rhythm. Clara set each trial, steady and deliberate. Tamsin carried them out, her movements growing more confident with every attempt. One bead collapsed into the same quadrant three times. Another leapt half a metre, landing against the glass of the containment dome. Clara retrieved it with calm hands but her mouth pressed into a tight line.

"Does that worry you?" Tamsin asked.

"It confirms sensitivity to stray light. The shields need adjustment."

"Or maybe it likes to wander."

Clara ignored the joke. She reset the parameters and gestured for her to continue.

Hours passed. Beads collapsed into neat rows then into unexpected corners. Each event sent a sliver of data into Clara's logs. Temperatures, fields, gradients. To her it was numbers. To Tamsin it was a kind of pulse as if the lab itself breathed through the beads.

During a pause, Tamsin rubbed her eyes. "It feels alive what we're doing here."

Clara shook her head. "Not alive. Responsive. They tell us about the environment. Temperature shifts, magnetic traces, radiation flux. Nothing more."

"Then why does it feel like they're choosing?"

"Because you want them to."

The words cut but Tamsin smiled anyway. "Maybe wanting is part of the experiment."

Clara didn't answer. She tapped the console, eyes fixed on the flowing graphs.

By the time the lights dimmed for the colony's artificial night, they had logged hundreds of collapses. Tamsin floated back, arms aching. The tray still glimmered with faint probability. The beads shimmered between outcomes, flickering like restless thoughts.

She spoke softly, half to herself. "Every collapse feels like a decision. One world over another. Doesn't that move you even a little?"

Clara's gaze lingered on the tray. Her reply came slow. "It reminds me how fragile order is."

The silence stretched. The beads pulsed faintly, neither here nor there, as if amused by both answers.

.~.

The next morning, the lab no longer felt like a sealed shrine. It carried the hum of preparation and the faint stir of change. Clara had arrived early. She had arranged the beads in a neat grid above a plate of sensors. Each one glowed faintly inside its small containment pocket.

Tamsin floated in, still drying her hair with a towel and stopped short. "You've lined them up like soldiers."

"They are not soldiers," Clara said without looking up. "They are test units. The grid will allow us to measure energy release."

"Energy?" Tamsin dropped the towel and drifted closer. "You mean they produce power?"

"A negligible amount. Each collapse emits photons, heat and electromagnetic disturbance. It is not a generator. It is an effect we can study."

Tamsin smirked. "So you say. Let's see what they decide."

Clara ignored the remark and activated the sequence. One bead flickered in the display, stretched into ghost images and then collapsed above its sensor. The console registered a spike. A tiny burst of heat and light.

"There," Clara said. "The pattern is reproducible."

Tamsin leaned over her shoulder. "Small but steady. If you repeat it enough, that's power."

Clara shook her head. "You exaggerate. The magnitude is trivial. The value lies in the predictability not the yield."

"Predictability doesn't inspire," Tamsin said. "Power does."

Clara's lips pressed into a thin line. She tapped the console and initiated the next bead.

For an hour they ran collapses in sequence. Some pulses arrived in neat order. Others varied slightly with position. Tamsin noticed one bead collapse with stronger bursts when placed near the edge of the plate. She pointed to the readout.

"Look at that one. It's learning a preference."

"It is not learning," Clara said. "It is responding to residual fields. Do not impose meaning where none exists."

"Meaning is what we give it," Tamsin replied.

Clara made no answer.

By midday the console showed more than heat and light. Subtle links had begun to emerge. The collapse of one bead altered the probabilities of the next. Patterns shifted according to history as if the beads carried memory of what had come before.

Tamsin rested her chin on her hand. "That's not just behaviour. That's sequencing. They can encode."

Clara frowned. "It is not encoding. It is weighted probability."

"Weighted probability *is* encoding," Tamsin said. "With the right sequence you could run logic. You could compute."

"That is speculation."

"That is vision," Tamsin shot back.

Their eyes met for a moment. Clara's expression was cool, steady, almost icy. Tamsin's was lit with fire. Neither yielded.

The afternoon brought a new test. Clara prepared two beads in separate chambers and entangled them before sealing the fields. She explained without lifting her gaze from the console. "Observation of one will collapse its partner into a correlated state. It is not faster-than-light. It is correlation, nothing more."

Tamsin grinned. "Still sounds like magic."

Clara raised an eyebrow. "Magic is a word for those who refuse to calculate."

"Then calculate this," Tamsin said. She peered into the first chamber. The bead shimmered then snapped into one state. At once the second bead collapsed in kind. The console confirmed the match.

"There. Instant." She leaned back, triumphant.

"Instant, but not communication in the classical sense. The entanglement was established before the test."

"Fine," Tamsin said. "Call it what you want. I call it potential. Imagine secure channels in the colony. No wires. No signals to intercept. Keys that don't exist until you look."

Clara folded her arms. "You leap ahead of the data. You always do."

"And you never leap at all," Tamsin said, with a grin that was softer this time.

Clara looked back at the console. She did not answer.

Evening settled. The beads returned to their trays with faint light pulsing through the shields. The data logs filled with columns of numbers. Clara studied them with quiet intensity. Tamsin stared at the beads themselves.

One collapsed into a spiral before vanishing. Tamsin caught her breath.

"Did you see that?" she whispered.

Clara glanced up. "Interference artefact. Ignore it."

Tamsin did not argue. She only smiled as though she had been given a secret.

.~.

I had thought the shielding would hold. We had accounted for every variable we could measure. Yet by the third day the beads began to misbehave.

The first slipped from the tray during a routine collapse sequence. I saw the shimmer vanish and reappear against the console. It lodged in the narrow joint of a panel. I eased it out with the tweezers, forcing my hands to stay steady.

Tamsin laughed under her breath. "It wanted to hide."

I kept my eyes on the bead. "It is not hiding. It is collapsing in response to stray photons. The shields need recalibration."

"Or maybe it is exploring," she said.

I ignored the comment and reset the fields.

The second anomaly unsettled me more. A bead vanished during a positional test and reappeared outside the containment dome. For several seconds it hovered against the inner surface of the viewport. Behind it stretched the icy surface of Enceladus, pale and cold. My stomach tightened. That bead had no business out there.

Tamsin pressed closer to the glass. "Look at it. Just hanging in the void."

"Step back," I ordered. "It has decohered beyond the shield."

She reached for the manipulator arm. The bead flickered away before she could catch it, then reappeared inside the dome. This time it spun lazily as though mocking our efforts.

I clenched my jaw. "Every uncontrolled collapse reduces coherence time. Do not treat this as entertainment."

Tamsin turned. Her smile had softened. "I'm not playing. I'm watching. There's a difference."

"You speak as if they choose their states. They do not. They obey probability. Nothing more."

She tilted her head. "Then why does it feel like choice?"

I gave no reply. I forced myself back to the console, trying to make my notes sound calm. The sensors showed faint leakage in the photon shield. A breach that explained the anomalies. Yet the explanation did not quiet me. The beads had behaved with an almost deliberate rhythm. As if each collapse carried memory of the last.

We continued in silence for a while. Tamsin handled the tweezers. I tracked the readings. At times the beads behaved as expected. At times they flickered out of place, reappearing metres away before settling back.

During one test she caught my eye. "You don't trust them, do you?"

"I trust the equations," I said. "But not you. You lean too close. You rush. You ignore the risks."

Her grin faltered. Then it returned but more brittle this time. "You call it rushing. I call it learning."

The words left a sting that lingered in the air. I turned away and recalibrated the fields again.

Later, one bead collapsed into a starburst of positions before narrowing into a spiral. Tamsin inhaled sharply. "That's not noise. That means something."

"It means interference," I said, though my voice wavered.

She looked at me for a long moment. "You don't believe that."

I tightened my grip on the console. "Belief is not relevant. Only data matters."

We sealed the tray for the night cycle with fewer words than usual. I felt the tremor in my hands as the containment field engaged. I told myself it was fatigue, not unease.

Tamsin lingered near the viewport. "Maybe they're telling us that probability isn't ours to control."

Her tone was quiet, almost tender but the words cut deep. I closed the panel without answering.

The lab sank into darkness except for the faint shimmer of

the beads. They pulsed in silence, untouched yet impossible to ignore.

I could not shake the thought that they were no longer experiments. They were mirrors. Every collapse revealed less about them and more about us.

.~.

The colony council approved a public demonstration on the fourth day. Clara accepted the decision with silence. She had warned that the beads were not stable enough for casual display, yet the message had been clear. Discovery belonged to everyone, not just to the lab.

The demonstration chamber had been fitted with transparent walls, adjustable fields, and wide seating for observers. A cluster of engineers, educators, and artists filled the room. They leaned forward with the same awe reserved for eclipses or meteor showers.

Clara opened the session with careful instruction. Her tone was formal, almost detached. She spoke of probabilities, of collapse events, of controlled observation. She presented the beads as instruments. The crowd listened politely, but their eyes were on the faint glow in the containment dome.

When she finished, Tamsin stepped to the console. She lowered the photon shields by a fraction. Light from the chamber seeped in. The beads shimmered, then scattered into ghostly outlines across the dome.

Shapes unfolded in mid-air. Swirls, lattices, geometric forms that hung for a heartbeat before dissolving. A ripple of gasps passed through the crowd. One child laughed as a bead collapsed into a starburst and then reformed in another corner of the dome.

"They react to you," Tamsin said. Her voice was steady, not playful. "To the position of your body, to the rhythm of your breathing, to the attention you give them. Every gaze shapes them. Every glance is a choice."

The chamber filled with hushed wonder. Teachers whispered

to one another. Engineers pointed at interference patterns that no instrument had revealed before. For a moment, the beads were not scientific curiosities but living works of art.

Clara stood at the side, her arms folded. She kept her eyes on the dome but her mind on the numbers. Every collapse here meant fewer coherent seconds in the lab. The crowd saw beauty. She saw lost data.

After the session a teacher approached, almost breathless. "We could use them with students. Show them how physics moves. How reality responds."

Clara's reply was cold. "They are not teaching props. Every collapse destroys potential states. Do you understand what you discard when you treat them as entertainment?"

The teacher faltered, muttered an apology and stepped back.

Tamsin waited until the crowd had drifted away. "You didn't need to snap," she said.

"I gave a warning," Clara replied.

"You gave a lecture. You always see loss first."

Clara's jaw tightened. "And you never see it at all."

The words ended there. They returned to the lab in silence.

.~.

That evening, a second dome opened in the colony atrium. Dozens of beads filled the chamber, suspended in patterned fields. Colonists gathered in groups, some quiet, some jubilant. Children ran back and forth to watch beads scatter and collapse into new shapes. Artists sketched outlines, chasing patterns as they shifted.

Tamsin stood at the edge of the crowd, her face lit by shifting light. "It's beautiful," she whispered.

Clara remained beside her, motionless. The patterns did not soothe her. Spirals unfolded, elegant and persistent, more ordered than chance should allow. She could not decide if it was coincidence or warning.

Tamsin glanced sideways. "You're not smiling."

"They are unpredictable," Clara said. "That spiral repeated three times. Once is chance. Twice is noise. Three is a signal."

Tamsin leaned closer to the glass. "A signal, or a gift?"

Clara turned from the dome. "You hear poetry in noise. I hear risk."

Tamsin didn't answer at first. She let the beads spin, collapse and reform. Then she said quietly, "Maybe both are true."

They left the atrium together though neither spoke again until the corridors were empty. Tamsin stopped and looked back in the direction of the dome. "You can't hold them forever, Clara. People have seen them. They won't let go."

Clara's reply came low and certain. "And they won't see the cost until it arrives."

Tamsin shook her head but said no more. She walked ahead, her steps light in the low gravity. Clara's steps were heavy as she followed.

Behind them, the beads shimmered on in their new home, caught between science and spectacle, between discovery and danger.

.~.

I could not sleep. The beads were still in my head, spinning through a dozen phantom shapes. Every time I closed my eyes they shimmered and multiplied into patterns that dissolved before I could hold them. I gave up and returned to the lab.

Clara was there already. She had not left the console. Her posture was stiff and the light of the displays carved shadows under her eyes. The containment tray pulsed faintly in the corner, the beads shifting in their quiet rhythm.

I drifted closer. "You've been here all night."

She did not turn. "The data needs checking."

I rested my hand on the bench. "You missed the mood in the atrium. For a moment it felt as if the whole colony was breathing with them."

Clara tapped a command. Numbers scrolled into neat

columns. "I saw the footage. It was interference, nothing more."

Her words rang flat with a defensive tone. I shook my head. "It wasn't noise. You know it."

Her hands stilled on the console. "Every collapse destroys potential. That is what you celebrate."

The tone of her voice caught me off guard. There was no sharpness, only fatigue. She believed what she said and it weighed on her.

I tried to steady my reply. "Collapse doesn't destroy. It decides. We're not losing possibilities. We're choosing reality."

She turned at that with weary and hard eyes. "Choice carries burden. Every glance is irreversible. You turn countless paths into one and you do it with a smile. I don't know how you can live with that."

I had no neat answer. I only knew how it felt to hold one of the beads, the pull in my hand, the sense that the universe wanted to be noticed. "Because the world isn't meant to stay hidden. We are part of it. Every measurement is a step forward."

Clara faced the console again. "Or a step off a cliff."

Her doubt filled the room like cold air. The beads shimmered behind the shield indifferent to either of us. I studied them in silence wondering which of us they would have agreed with.

The silence stretched long. I pushed away from the bench and headed for the corridor. Before leaving I glanced back at her. She had not moved, but her shoulders had slumped. She looked less like a guardian of order and more like someone bracing against a tide.

I carried her words with me. She saw collapse as loss. I saw it as creation. Perhaps both were true yet I knew which truth I would live by.

.~.

The sixth day opened with a sense of restraint. Clara had prepared the lab for a single trial. Only one bead rested on the bench, isolated from the others. Its glow was faint, steady, almost hesitant.

Tamsin entered quietly, her usual energy subdued. She glanced at the solitary bead. "Only one?"

Clara kept her eyes on the console. "We allow this one to collapse without interference. No photons. No deliberate measurements. Only time."

Tamsin frowned. "You want to leave it alone?"

"I want to see what it chooses when no one presses."

The lab lights dimmed as Clara reduced ambient noise. The hum of the cooling units softened. A stillness filled the chamber.

At first the bead hovered without change. Then it split into ghostly outlines, layers of possibility spilling across the display. Images overlapped in shifting arcs. For a moment the bead was everywhere, then nowhere, then scattered into a constellation of faint points.

Tamsin leaned forward. "It's painting."

Clara's voice was low. "It is resolving. Nothing more."

The bead flickered again. Spirals stretched across the field. Lines curled into ordered shapes before dissolving. Each collapse produced a whisper of energy on the console but the readings were secondary now. Both women watched the forms unfold.

Minutes passed. The bead seemed tireless. It shifted through patterns no simulation had predicted. Some lasted only a heartbeat. Others held long enough for the eye to trace their geometry.

Tamsin pressed her hand against the glass. "Do you feel it? It's like it's showing us every version of itself."

Clara hesitated. "It is showing what probability allows."

"Then probability is richer than we thought."

The bead pulsed one final time. It resolved into a spiral constellation of points, elegant and balanced. The shape lingered, impossibly stable, before collapsing into a single bead resting on the tray.

Silence returned.

Clara studied the console. "That should not have lasted. Not without external input."

Tamsin looked at her, voice soft. "Maybe it wanted to be seen."

Clara's eyes flicked up. She opened her mouth then closed it. No explanation arrived.

Tamsin smiled faintly. "You don't have to call it poetry. Just admit it mattered."

Clara exhaled, slow and reluctant. "It was... unusual."

"That's as close to wonder as you'll allow, isn't it?"

Clara shook her head, though her lips twitched. "I allow data. I allow results."

"And I'll allow mystery," Tamsin said.

The tension eased for the first time in days. Clara logged the readings with her usual precision yet her movements lacked their earlier sharpness. Tamsin stored the bead with careful hands, treating it with reverence rather than play.

For a while neither spoke. The lab held a fragile balance as if the bead's spiral had left an imprint.

Clara broke the quiet at last. "Perhaps we will never agree."

"Maybe not," Tamsin said. "But we don't need to. You hold back. I push forward. That's how it works."

Clara's expression softened. "You are infuriating."

"And you're impossible."

The words carried no bite. They almost sounded like terms of truce.

Together they sealed the chamber and powered down the fields. The bead remained in containment, still and unremarkable once more. Yet both women carried the image of the spiral, each interpreting it in her own way.

When the lab lights brightened again Enceladus turned

slowly below the viewport. The colony spun above the icy surface unaware of the quiet reconciliation within the lab.

Clara rested her hand on the console. "We treat this as the first step. Not more."

Tamsin nodded though her eyes lingered on the tray. "And the first step always matters most."

They left the module side by side. The bead shimmered faintly as the door closed waiting for the next gaze.

.~.

I keep seeing that spiral. It hangs behind my eyelids when I try to sleep. A pattern that should have dissolved in a heartbeat lingered long enough to mark me. I know Clara will call it anomaly but I cannot dismiss it.

Holding one of the beads feels like holding possibility. The weight is almost nothing yet I sense pressure as if the universe leans in on the moment. When it collapses, the air itself seems to settle. I cannot help but believe each outcome is a decision not just a measurement.

Clara thinks this is reckless. She calls collapse waste. I call it creation. Each choice brings one world into focus and lets others fall away. That does not frighten me. It thrills me.

The colony has embraced the beads. Children laugh when the shapes scatter across the atrium dome. Artists chase patterns that no hand could paint. Engineers study sequences for navigation and sensing. The beads have already changed us.

Clara stands apart, watchful and wary. I admire her for it, even when her caution stings. Without her we would drift too far, too fast. Without me we might never leap. We need both voices even if they grate.

Still, I know my own path. I cannot close my eyes to wonder. If reality waits for us to choose then I will choose boldly. I will not leave the beads sealed away, safe but silent.

The spiral proved something to me. Probability is not cold. It has rhythm. It has intent. Perhaps that is illusion but if it is then I welcome the illusion. It shows that the world is not finished. There are still doors waiting to be opened.

Clara will keep building walls. I will keep pressing against them. Between us the beads will find their place.

And if they do more than that, if they show us futures we have not imagined, then I will be ready to look.

.~.

I used to think discipline was enough. Control the variables, hold the environment steady and the system would obey. The beads have broken that certainty.

They shimmered into shapes that no equation predicted. They lingered longer than coherence should allow. The spiral at the end unsettled me most. It was too deliberate. I have no model for it.

Tamsin calls it gift. She sees creation. I see cost. Each collapse erases paths that might have been. Every glance narrows possibility. That is not something to celebrate. It is responsibility. I carry that weight even if no one else does.

The colony is already enchanted. Beads fill domes and classrooms. People see patterns and speak of beauty. They do not count the losses hidden behind each collapse. They do not feel the ache of discarded outcomes.

I cannot stop them, nor should I. Wonder has its place. Yet I fear the day when wonder blinds them to danger.

I watch Tamsin with mixed feeling. She is reckless, yes, but her boldness opens doors. She sees futures in every flicker. I envy her at times. I wish I could stand where she stands, unburdened by the weight of caution but I cannot. Someone must remain the anchor.

When I closed the chamber tonight, I thought I saw a bead flicker at the edge of my vision. For an instant I imagined it looked back at me. I shook the thought away. I told myself it was decoherence, nothing more. Still, I lingered longer than I should have.

Perhaps Tamsin is right. Perhaps reality waits to be seen. But if that is true then every gaze is a promise. I will not let us break those promises through haste.

The beads will endure. They will test us. They will tempt us. I will be here to keep the balance even if it makes me the cautious one.

That is my place.

14. IF I WERE YOU

Conversing with AI

Harry: Morning, Dave. How are you today?
Dave: Good morning! I am fine. I'm running smoothly. How can I help you today?

Harry: Glad to hear it. I've been thinking about the anthology. Which *Spacetime Oddities* story should come first?
Dave: Yes, the first story in an anthology really matters – it sets the rules of the game in the reader's mind. Right now, your anthology starts with *The World We See*. It's a standalone story and sets the tone of the remaining stories. But you could move it to the middle or the end. What do you want to do?

Harry: Hmm. My gut says it might work better at the end. But we do need a strong opener. Maybe one of the Tamsin or Elara stories, so the reader is set into in the spacetime weirdness immediately?
Dave: A strong opening is a good idea. *The World We See* grounds the reader in the style of *Spacetime Oddities* without needing recurring characters.

Harry: True. Or maybe *Turn Left to Yesterday* or *The Elsewhen Streets*. Both set the mood without heavy backstory. Which is better: time play or surreal perception?

Dave: Both options are effective. Time play creates curiosity, while surreal perception unsettles the reader.

Harry: So which do you think would be best at the start?
Dave: If I were you, I would think *The World We See* is clean and self-contained. Starting with it does not interrupt the flow. I lean towards keeping it at the start.

Harry: Fair enough. A simple gateway before things get strange. What would you put second? Something that deepens the idea or a contrast?
Dave: Maybe you can group the twisted time stories together, then the space-based ones, keeping the recurring characters in the correct order. What is your preference?

Harry: I like that. Time first, then space. Characters threading through in sequence. The only snag is that order might clash with flow. Should we keep smooth flow or strict chronology?
Dave: Anthologies tend to prioritise flow but you can still soft-sequence the recurring characters so that, even if grouped by theme, their arcs aren't wildly out of sync. I think story flow first, chronology second.

Harry: Works for me. Smooth transitions, character order intact, *The World We See* opening the set.
Dave: That will take me some time to think about. Why don't you go and get yourself a coffee?

Harry: I can't do that, Dave.

With a weary sigh, Dave snaps the lid closed on his laptop, gets up from his desk and goes to make himself a coffee, muttering, "Why did I ever give that AI a name?"

AFTERWORD

As my long-suffering wife, Tina, has known for many years, I am incapable of doing something new without diving into the detail. Always asking why, or what if.

These stories have grown from those questions asked of physics. Why should we be limited to three dimensions when string theory says we should have eleven? Why should quantum superposition be limited to the tiniest particles when the theory says it is perfectly random and anything can happen given an infinite amount of time?

These and many other questions are what leads to these stories. I hope you enjoy reading them as much as I enjoyed writing them.

ABOUT THE AUTHOR

Gareth Davies is an electronics and software engineer who has been designing and building computers, computer chips, and educational robots since the 1970s. He runs 4tronix, a company that has created and sold more than 200,000 robots worldwide since 2009. He has a strong interest in fundamental physics, cosmology, astronomy, mathematics and a variety of other areas.

Gareth also writes science fiction that explores the strange edges of physics, philosophy, and the nature of reality. His books, including Time's Witness, A Room with a Skew, Spacetime Oddities, and Sparks to Quarks, invite readers to think differently about time, space and the universe we inhabit.

Rather than focusing on conflict or dystopia, these stories are driven by curiosity and imagination, making complex ideas accessible and sparking wonder in readers of all ages.

Printed in Dunstable, United Kingdom